"Thank you for trusting me, Spider. I won't betray you," Anne said, touching his upper arm.

"I know you won't," he answered. When she touched him, he thought his heart was going to rip itself out it was pounding so hard. The flowery smell of Anne, the soft feel of her had worked itself into his pores. At that moment he'd have given everything he owned to kiss her.

He tried to tell himself to pull away, but he felt as if the whole Pittsburgh Steelers team had piled on top of him. He ached to taste her, just once.

Anne stood spellbound, fascinated by the contour of his lips, with the line that creased the lower one and divided it into two curves, sensuous and full. How soft, how warm his lips would feel.

His face moved toward hers in a maddening, gradual descent, as if pulled by the force of longing inside her. His eyes glittered like blue crystals, and he drew closer, her lids fluttered shut and her hand pressed and moved across the solid expanse of his chest.

"Oh, darlin'," he groaned, and his mouth captured hers with a consuming power that stole the strength from her bones. . . .

WHAT ARE *LOVESWEPT* ROMANCES?

They are stories of true romance and touching emotion. We believe those two very important ingredients are constants in our highly sensual and very believable stories in the *LOVESWEPT* line. Our goal is to give you, the reader, stories of consistently high quality that may sometimes make you laugh, sometimes make you cry, but are always fresh and creative and contain many delightful surprises within their pages.

Most romance fans read an enormous number of books. Those they truly love, they keep. Others may be traded with friends and soon forgotten. We hope that each *LOVESWEPT* romance will be a treasure—a "keeper." We will always try to publish

LOVE STORIES YOU'LL NEVER FORGET
BY AUTHORS YOU'LL ALWAYS REMEMBER

The Editors

LOVESWEPT® • 397

Jan Hudson
Step Into My Parlor

BANTAM BOOKS
NEW YORK • TORONTO • LONDON • SYDNEY • AUCKLAND

STEP INTO MY PARLOR

A Bantam Book / May 1990

*LOVESWEPT® and the wave device are registered
trademarks of Bantam Books, a division of
Bantam Doubleday Dell Publishing Group, Inc.
Registered in U.S. Patent
and Trademark Office and elsewhere.*

*If you would be interested in receiving protective vinyl
covers for your Loveswept books, please write to this address
for information:*

Loveswept
Bantam Books
P.O. Box 985
Hicksville, NY 11802

ISBN 0-553-44025-X

Published simultaneously in the United States and Canada

---

*Bantam Books are published by Bantam Books, a division
of Bantam Doubleday Dell Publishing Group, Inc. Its trademark, consisting of the words "Bantam Books" and the
portrayal of a rooster, is Registered in U.S. Patent and
Trademark Office and in other countries. Marca Registrada.
Bantam Books, 666 Fifth Avenue, New York, New York 10103.*

PRINTED IN THE UNITED STATES OF AMERICA

OPM   Q 9 8 7 6 5 4 3 2

For my friend Jan Milella,
who loves a good chase.

One

Be home, be home, Anne willed as she listened to the phone ring for the fifth time. She'd used her last quarter, and all that was left in her wallet were three pennies and a dozen useless credit cards.

"This is Victoria Chase," the recorded voice said. "I'm sorry I can't answer your call, but if you'll leave your name—"

Anne slammed the receiver down and leaned her head against the telephone. She needed to talk to Vicki. The past two weeks had been a nightmare, and Vicki was her last hope. Even though she didn't think that her stepbrother, Preston Ames, would look for her in Houston, she couldn't chance leaving her name. Preston was a desperate man with powerful connections. She wouldn't feel safe until he was locked away. But first, she had to convince somebody that her accusations against him weren't simply some sort of delusional grief reaction to her mother's death.

Cars and trucks whizzed by the corner gas station where Anne stood, pouring their noise and noxious fumes into the chill night wind that tugged at the opening of her sable coat. Their frantic pace, their overwhelming impersonality added to the panic clawing at her insides. Other than Vicki, she didn't know a soul in Houston.

A wave of nausea billowed over her, and the headache she'd been fighting erupted full force. Exhausted, dejected, she turned up the collar of her coat against the early February cold and trudged back to her white Jaguar. Teeth chattering, she started the engine and turned on the heater. The soft music on the car radio did nothing to soothe her despair.

A hotel sign from the Galleria, just beyond Neiman Marcus, taunted her. Another, across the freeway, shimmered and beckoned with promises of a comfortable bed and warm food. She was almost tempted to succumb to their allure. She hadn't eaten since she'd traded her garnet ring for dinner the night before in a little cafe somewhere in Louisiana, and she hated to spend another miserable night in the car. But she knew that using credit cards would divulge her location to Preston's trackers. She'd made that mistake twice, with nearly disastrous results.

Her body buzzed with weariness and her nerves were strung taut with tension; her stomach cramped and rumbled. And the hotel signs glittered and teased and whispered enticements in her mind.

Temptation almost overwhelmed her. Snatching up her manicure scissors and her wallet, she yanked the gold and silver and blue cards from their slots. She whacked and sawed and cut them into tiny pieces. When the last one was reduced to plastic confetti littering the plush interior of the car, she leaned her head back with a moaning sigh. Now what?

What was she going to do?

"Friend," a deep voice on the radio drawled, "are you a little short of cash?"

Anne let out a whimpering, bitter sound that fell far short of a laugh. "Short of cash and out of options."

"Well, ol' Spider knows that feeling," the voice said. "And I'd like to help you out. Grab something of value you've got laying around the house to use as collateral and get what you need to tide you over. We'll make loans on jewelry, boats, guns, or just about anything you can name. Even your prize bull or your mother-in-law's false teeth. Spider Webb's Pawn Parlor. I'm on Richmond, just a couple of blocks behind the Galleria. Call if you're bashful—or come on by. I'm open till nine every night. Spider Webb's Pawn Parlor, 555-4653."

A loan. Of course. She felt for the watch on her arm and her mother's pearls around her neck. No, she couldn't part with the pearls, but maybe she could get enough from the watch for a hotel room and gas for the car. Surely she would be able to contact Vicki by tomorrow.

After securing directions from the station attendant, she drove toward her destination. In a few minutes, she saw the red neon sign, bordered by a row of rippling lights, and pulled into the small strip shopping center. It was almost nine o'clock; she prayed that the shop would still be open.

After she killed the engine, she sat staring at the bar-covered plate-glass windows, which displayed a melange of musical instruments, tools, and assorted other items people had traded for cash. She'd seen places like this in movies, but she'd never been in such an establishment in her life. How ironic that Anne Foxworth Jennings, the heiress to the luxurious Royal Fox Hotels, was reduced to pawning her watch for a place to sleep.

Taking a deep breath to fortify her courage, she gathered her shoulder bag and the briefcase that had rarely left her sight in the past two weeks, got out, locked the Jaguar, and walked to the door.

It was locked, and she almost panicked. Then she noticed a sign and an arrow pointing to a button. Her leather-gloved finger trembling, she pushed the buzzer and heard a click. She opened the door and went into the shop, which was filled with shelves bulging with every imaginable item. She could hear the noise of a television broadcast somewhere in the rear of the large room.

"Step into my parlor, sweet thing."

Startled, Anne's head swung to her right, and her eyes searched the area where she'd heard the strange, mellow voice.

But she saw nothing except a tapestry-covered Victorian settee in front of shelves of televisions, stereos, tape decks, and speakers.

"Step into my parlor, sweet thing." A peculiar, eerie laugh followed. "Let ol' Spider help you out."

Her eyes widened and she sucked in a quick breath.

"Don't mind Turk, sugar," another man's voice drawled from the back of the shop. "He's my watch bird. Come on in."

"Come on in," the mellow voice echoed.

When Anne spied the myna sitting in a large cage behind the settee, she relaxed. Slightly.

"Hot damn! In for two. Way to go, Akeem!" the one at the back yelled.

"Hot damn," the myna agreed.

Anne froze in her tracks. Heart pounding and fear creeping up into her throat, she couldn't have moved an inch if the building were on fire.

"Damn! My main man mopped up the floor with Bullets." The TV clicked off. "Don't be shy, sugar. Come on back. We slaughtered 'em and ol' Spider is feeling generous tonight."

She swallowed. What had she gotten herself into? Everything in her screamed to turn and run. She didn't need money that badly.

Then her stomach rumbled and she remembered the three lone pennies in her purse. Yes she did. She took a fortifying breath and reached down deep for an extra measure of courage.

Picking her way around a drum set, a riding lawn mower, and a tall wooden Indian, she headed toward the back of the long room.

Three large glass cases, filled with handguns and jewelry, stretched across the back of the shop. Leaning against one of the cases was a man. A big man. A swarthy, rough-looking man. Arms crossed and the fingers of his huge hands tucked under his armpits, he leaned one hip against the glass and looked her up and down.

Anne nearly fainted. This was not the type of man with whom she ordinarily associated. Although he appeared to be only a few years older than she, his whole demeanor spoke of a dozen lifetimes' more experience.

He was at least six-feet-four, with shoulders a yard wide. He wore black boots, black jeans, a black T-shirt, and a black leather jacket with silver zippers and brads. The leather of his jacket was so worn in places that it looked as if the garment should have been thrown away five years ago. His hair, black, thick, and slightly curly, was short on top and on the sides but hung past his collar in the back. The lower part of his face was shadowed by several days' growth of heavy beard and outlined a mouth with a gently curving upper lip and a full lower one. An old, slightly jagged scar cut across one high cheekbone. A miniature silver cutlass dangled from his left ear.

If she'd met him in a dark alley, Anne would have turned and fled screaming into the night. She wouldn't have noticed his eyes in a dark alley. But it was light, and beneath the thick slash of black eyebrows, his eyes paralyzed her. Surrounded by long, curly lashes, they were totally incongruous with the rest of his menacing appearance.

They were blue. Light blue. The blue of a summer sky or the shallows of the Mediterranean. And they were all over her. She could feel them.

And she could feel something else emanating from him. It was raw. And primal. And earthy. It pulsated from him like body heat. It surrounded her and plucked at some primitive level that slithered in her belly and rippled over her body. She had the strangest urge to growl and bare her teeth and circle like a wild animal in a mating ritual. The feeling shocked her. And it terrified her.

He licked his lips. She licked hers.

"I . . . I . . ."

One corner of his sensual mouth lifted. "You need a little cash tonight, hon?" He moved toward her.

She swallowed and stepped back.

"Hell, sugar, that's no sin. I've been short a few times myself. Let's see what you got."

"My watch." She set the briefcase down and fumbled with the clasp at her wrist.

"Here, let me do that."

His big hands were surprisingly gentle as he bent to the task. And the scent of him filled her nostrils. He smelled of citrus and sandalwood and virile male. She closed her eyes and held her breath as she slid the watch and safety chain over her fingers.

"Niiice," his deep voice drawled. "Very nice."

She felt him move away and opened her eyes. He had gone behind the case. He laid the diamond-and-gold watch on a square of black velvet and picked up a jeweler's loupe.

After he'd looked at the watch for a moment, he said, "Loan or sell?"

"Pardon?"

He smiled a knowing smile. "Do you want to borrow money on the watch or do you want to sell it outright?"

She fiddled with the strap of her purse. "Loan, I suppose. How much may I borrow?"

"Three-thirty is the max."

"Only three thousand and thirty dollars. But it cost over—"

"No, sugar." He smiled again. "Three *hundred* and thirty dollars. I know what one of these babies is worth, but the way the state law is set up, we can only afford to loan three-thirty max on any one item. Sorry."

Anne rubbed her head with her fingertips. What choice did she have? She had to eat and she had to find a place to sleep until she could contact Vicki.

"May I use your phone before I decide?" She'd call Vicki one last time.

"Sure." He gestured to a telephone at the end of one of the cases.

She punched out the numbers and waited. "This is Victoria Chase. I'm sorry I—"

Anne hung up and turned to Spider Webb, who was leaning back, hands under his armpits again, watching her. Light caught the silver cutlass dangling from his ear and she shivered. He reminded her of a pirate or the leader of one of those barbarous motorcycle gangs. He made her very nervous, but she had no choice except to deal with him. She sighed. "Three-thirty."

She felt his eyes drop to the V of her beige silk blouse, and a flush crept up her neck. Her first impulse was to clutch her coat around her throat, but, instead, she raised her chin and walked back to the counter where he stood. "I'll take the three hundred and thirty dollars."

His eyes remained at the V. "I can give you another three-thirty for the pearls."

"My pearls?" Her hand flew to the opera-length strand, and she seized them with nervous fingers. "No, not my pearls." She tucked them inside her blouse and was comforted by their familiar warmth against her skin.

His gaze traveled higher. "Fifty for the earrings."

Her hand went to the gold loop in her right ear. They had been a gift from her stepfather on her sixteenth birthday. The last thing he'd given her before his death eleven years ago. She shook her head. "Just the watch."

He shrugged, pulled out a ticket, and picked up a pen. "Name?"

"Anne . . . Smith."

He looked at her, raised a dark eyebrow, then wrote it down. "Address?"

She gave him Vicki's address.

"You have some ID?"

"ID?" Panic began bubbling in the pit of her stomach.

"Identification. You know, like a driver's license, passport, something like that. Law says we gotta see some ID."

She fidgeted with her purse, trying desperately to think of a reason why her driver's license and passport would have a different name from the one she'd given him. Pulling her wallet from her bag, she opened it, took out her license, and handed it to him.

"Uh . . . Smith is my maiden name. Jennings is—was—my husband's name. We're separated. Divorced," she amended quickly. "And I don't live in Virginia anymore. I'm moving in with my friend in Houston. I haven't had time to change my license."

He looked at the license and the picture for a long time. Then he looked up at her. His blue eyes intense, yet filled with something that seemed like compassion, he asked softly, "Was he mean to you, sugar?"

"Pardon?"

"Your husband, this dude you're running from— was he mean to you?"

There was such gentleness in his eyes, in his tone, that her throat constricted. She pursed her lips and gave a quick nod.

"It's gonna be okay, darlin'." He patted her hand. Counting out the cash in fifties, twenties, and tens, he said, "The loan is for thirty days. Twenty percent interest. You have a sixty-day grace period, then the watch becomes mine. If you can't redeem it by then, you can come by and pay the interest to hold it another thirty days."

She gave another nod and reached for the money.

"And, sugar," he added, covering her slender hand with his big one, "if you need some more cash and decide to sell the watch, come see ol' Spider. I'll give you a better deal than anybody in town."

"Thank you," she managed to whisper. She

stuffed the bills and license in her wallet and dropped it in her shoulder bag. Turning, she walked quickly from the shop.

Once outside, she breathed in a large gulp of cold night air. It hurt her lungs and smelled of exhaust fumes, but she sucked in another shuddering breath, then fumbled for her car keys. Tonight, at least, she would eat a decent meal and sleep in a comfortable bed. Tonight, at least, she would be safe. Tomorrow she would locate Vicki, and her friend would know how to stop Preston.

Just as she pushed the key in the Jaguar's lock and turned it, something hard was shoved against her back. A hand jerked her bag from her shoulder, and a menacing voice behind her growled, "Don't move, lady. I've got a gun."

Two

"You be careful out there, sugar," Spider had called behind her, but she hadn't heard. She was already out the door.

Class. That little lady had class. It was the kind of class his ex-wife Janine had craved but could never quite pull off—not even with the big money he'd made when he was playing pro ball. It wasn't the Russian sable he'd estimated at forty grand or the Italian boots or the fancy French purse or any of the expensive clothes she wore that made her classy. She had the kind of class that was bred in and showing by the time a kid was out of diapers.

She was a looker, too. Even with her brown hair skinned back in one of those knots like the ballet dancers wore and dark circles under her eyes, she had a pretty face. Good bones. A nice mouth. And a cute little nose. And soft brown eyes that reminded him of Bambi.

Yeah, she was one fine lady. He'd known her name wasn't Smith, but he hadn't had the heart to call her on it. He figured the watch was not hot, so what did it matter? She was scared, and she was running from her husband. He'd seen enough of them come into the Parlor to recognize the signs.

He shook his head. That jerk she was married to ought to have his head examined. Lord, if he had a sweet thing like her for a wife, she wouldn't be hundreds of miles from home hocking her watch. When he thought of her scared and alone, his protective nature rose up, and he uttered a choice expletive he'd learned before he started kindergarten. Turk echoed his sentiment.

Checking his watch, Spider saw it was after nine. He decided to lock up for the night when he noticed the briefcase on the floor. She'd forgotten it.

Maybe he could catch her. He grabbed the case and loped to the front door. That's when he heard her scream.

Yanking open the door, he saw Anne struggling with a man by a white Jag. "Hey!" he yelled, dropping the briefcase and charging toward them.

The guy flung her to the pavement and leveled his gun at Spider. "Back off, man, or your brains are gone!"

Spider stopped and raised his hands, palms out and shoulder high. He looked from Anne, who lay sprawled on the ground crying, to the man holding her purse and fur coat. He could see that the robber was wild-eyed and nervous. "We don't want no trouble, buddy. Take what you got and go."

The thief tossed the coat and bag in the car, and, switching the gun to his left hand, yanked the keys from the door and got in the Jag. When he peeled out of the parking lot, Spider ran to Anne.

He squatted down beside her and raised her up. A scrape on her forehead, just above her right eyebrow, was bleeding. "Sugar, are you okay?"

She clutched the front of his leather jacket and sobbed. "He took the money. He took my car. He took everything I own. Now I don't even have a place to sleep."

"Ah, darlin', it'll be all right." He folded her in his arms and patted her back as she wept against his chest. "Come on inside with me. We'll call the police, and they'll probably catch him in a few minutes."

"No!" Anne cried, pulling back with a terrified look in her eyes. "You can't call the police."

"But, darlin', we have to report—"

Grabbing the lapels of his jacket, she pleaded, "No, please, please, don't call the police. Preston will find me, and he'll kill me." Her face was dead white.

"Sugar, the police will protect you. They won't let him hurt you."

"But you don't understand. Preston and his friends are very powerful. I'm not safe from him anywhere. Not even with the police. If he finds me, he'll kill me. I heard him. Nobody will listen to me, but I heard him. I swear it's the truth. You've got to believe me."

He gathered her in his long arms and held her

close. He could feel her shaking. "Shhh, darlin'. I believe you. We won't call the police. You come inside with me. O'l Spider won't let him hurt you."

He felt her relax against him, and he laid his cheek on the top of her head. She smelled like flowers.

Lifting her as if she weighed nothing, he carried her inside the pawnshop. If he could have gotten his hands on Preston right then, he would have decked him. Or worse. Spider had been dealing with slimeballs like him for most of his thirty-four years. After all, his father had been the biggest slimeball of them all.

The first thing Anne saw when she awakened was the head of a wild boar. It had on a baseball cap, sunglasses, and a tie and was mounted on the wall alongside what, if she wasn't mistaken, was an original LeRoy Neiman painting of clashing football players.

The next thing she noticed was that the pillow her cheek rested on smelled of citrus and sandalwood and virile male. Her eyes widened and she sat up with a start. She was in the middle of a huge brass bed that was in a roomful of the strangest assortment of furnishings she'd ever seen.

A mahogany Chippendale tall-case clock sat between an outboard motor and a scarred pump organ. An eighteenth-century Venetian armoire rested next to a lead birdbath, a racing bike, and two sets of water skis. The bedside lamp was

Tiffany, but it sat on a wooden packing crate. Her pearls lay at the base of the lamp.

Where was she? How had she ended up in a brass bed with red satin sheets and a fake fur spread? Was this some kind of bizarre dream? She looked down at herself.

Dear Lord, she wore a silk chemise and lace panties. And nothing else.

"Good morning," a deep voice said. "I thought I heard you stir."

Anne jerked the sheets up to her chin as Spider Webb came striding into the room with a tray. The black leather jacket was gone, but, except for a light blue T-shirt advertising Sea World, he was dressed as he was the night before. The blue T-shirt matched his eyes and clung to his muscled torso like plastic wrap. She was hard-pressed not to stare.

"Where am I? How did I get here?"

He grinned. "Don't you remember? You're at my Pawn Parlor."

"You *live* here?"

"Sure," he said, settling the bed tray over her lap. "Saves on insurance and it's as good a place as any. This part of the store used to be a pizza place. When they went broke, I took over the space. Some nights I swear I can still smell pepperoni. Sleep good?"

She nodded.

"Great. You were pretty well out of juice when I carried you in last night. I brought you some breakfast." He lifted the silver cover from a plate with four slices of bacon and two soft fried eggs.

The plate and coffee cup were Limoges. The silver was Francis I, and the orange juice glass was plastic. The salt and pepper shakers looked like the ones used by a major airline. Two biscuits sat in a small basket lined with a paper towel, but the yellow rose beside the basket was in a Lalique bud vase. Anne picked up the rose and smelled it.

Spider grinned. "I got it at the florist next door."

She smiled. "Thank you." She set it down and frowned as he stood beside the bed with his fingers tucked under his armpits.

"Aren't you hungry? Is something wrong with the food? I make bacon and eggs okay, but I sent one of the guys down to the chicken place for the biscuits. They're usually pretty good."

"It looks delicious, and I'm starving, but . . ." She gave him a pained look.

She waited for him to leave so that she could have some privacy. But he continued to stand beside the bed holding the tray. "I'm not dressed."

One of those thick black brows lifted, and he gave her a look that sucked the air from her lungs. "There's no need to be shy, sugar. I'm the one who put you to bed."

He settled the tray over her lap and removed the silver dome. "I hope it's still warm."

Although she was unmoved by his presence, she took a bite of food. "Perfect."

Spider felt his chest swell.

"Aren't you having breakfast?"

"I've already eaten." He'd devoured three earlier batches that had grown cold waiting for her to wake up, and he was about as full of eggs as he wanted to be.

He unfolded a step stool that was leaning against a wall in a corner, sat down, and watched her go after the bacon and eggs. Although her manners were pure Emily Post, she ate as if she were hungry. She'd probably missed a meal or two.

Hanging his boot heels over a rung of the stool, he propped his elbows on his knees, and, lacing his fingers together, sat and watched her butter a biscuit. He decided she looked so cute sitting in his bed with the sheets pulled primly under her chin and daintily munching on the biscuit that it was hard not to crawl in with her and feed her every bite.

One strap of her chemise slid from her smooth shoulder, and his gaze watched its slow descent. She had the prettiest skin. It looked as soft as a baby's bottom. He remembered the feel of it from when he'd taken off her clothes the night before. And he remembered sweet little curves. And long sleek legs. Lord, how good those—

With a shake of his head, he stopped his thoughts, and his feet hit the floor. What was he thinking? She was married.

Even though she wasn't wearing a wedding ring—and he'd checked it out last night after her gloves were off—he'd seen the faint mark where one had been. Separated? Maybe. But she wasn't divorced. Divorced women didn't run scared. Or have to hock a diamond watch when they were wearing Russian sables and driving Jags. She'd have gotten a hefty settlement if she'd divorced this Preston character.

She might be married to a first-class jerk, but

he had one unshakable rule. Spider Webb didn't mess with married women. Ever.

"I'll get you some more coffee."

"I've had plenty, but thank you." She smiled and it stopped him in his tracks. "Somehow you look different this morning." Tilting her head to one side, she drew her brows together and studied him with her large brown eyes. "I know. You've shaved your beard."

His hand went to his jaw. "It's Saturday."

"Saturday?"

He grinned. "I shave every Saturday, whether I need it or not."

She laughed. He'd never heard her laugh. It was a throaty, sexy sound that shimmied up his backbone. If he didn't beat a fast exit, her effect on him would have him reconsidering his cardinal rule.

"Thanks for the breakfast. And thank you for taking me in last night. I don't know what I would have done without your help."

"No problem, sugar. It's part of Texas hospitality." He took the tray. "Your clothes got pretty messed up in the parking lot. I took them to the cleaners this morning and told them it was a rush job. I'll check to see if they're ready."

"Now I have something else to thank you for. As soon as I'm dressed, I'll call my friend Vicki. Since it's Saturday, she's sure to be home. I'll ask her to pick me up, and I'll be out of your way."

"You're not in my way, darlin'." His gaze slid over the length of her. The red satin sheets hugged her body like a lover, outlining every dip and curve.

His fingers curled around the handles of the tray. "There's an extra toothbrush in the medicine cabinet. And I put your briefcase at the foot of the bed."

Anne slumped back against the pillows with a sigh of relief. "Thank you." And thank heaven, she thought as she heard the door close.

Her briefcase was the most important thing she owned. She'd been so distracted that she had forgotten it held her hope of survival. As long as she had it and was able to stay out of Preston's reach, she had a chance. The files in the case were the key to unmasking his corrupt plans. That and Vicki's assistance.

She climbed out of bed and went into the small bathroom to shower. As she unwound her long hair, she glimpsed herself in the mirror of the medicine cabinet and touched the bandage on her forehead. Spider must have put it there.

For someone who looked so menacing, Spider Webb was really a very gentle man. And rather attractive without the beard. Handsome in a rough kind of way. Incredibly . . . sensual. There was an elemental virility about him that affected her at a deep, visceral level. The feeling made her uneasy. Very uneasy.

He was not like any men she'd ever met. Not that her experience with men was all that vast. She'd been a late bloomer, more interested in horses than boys as a teenager. The Swiss boarding school where she'd met Vicki had been very strict and gave her little opportunity to learn much about the opposite sex.

Maybe that was why she'd fallen so hard for Dwayne Palmer in college. And why she'd been so hurt to discover that he was more interested in the Foxworth-Jennings millions than in her. After that devastating experience, she'd shielded her heart carefully.

While she hadn't become a social recluse or embittered with males in general, her subsequent relationships had been infrequent and with men of similar background. In fact, for the past few years, between her new business and caring for her mother, she hadn't had much time for a social life.

Elizabeth Ames, Anne's mother and Preston's stepmother, had always been a fragile, dependent type. Shortly after Anne had finished graduate school and had started her art gallery in Washington, D.C., her mother's delicate health had begun to deteriorate. Although Preston had lived in the household and managed Elizabeth's financial affairs for several years, Anne didn't want to trust the supervision of her mother's care to Preston or the servants, so she had moved back home to the Virginia suburb and had commuted to the gallery.

Almost every spare moment had been spent at her mother's bedside, reading to her, handling correspondence, or simply talking with the gentle woman. Although the past three years had been exhausting, Anne hadn't considered her task a sacrifice. She had adored her mother. But except for a few dinners at the club or a party once in a while, there was neither time nor energy left over for thoughts of men or romance.

In fact, Anne had been stunned when only a few days after Elizabeth's death, Preston had declared his love for her and asked her to marry him. She'd never considered the slightly paunchy, graying man, who was almost twenty years her senior, anything more than a stepbrother. Preston was . . . well, Preston was just Preston. In fact, she'd always thought him rather cold.

Now she understood why the ambitious conniver had always been so protective of her. It wasn't brotherly concern. Or his own undeclared love. He was simply guarding the goose for his own selfish purposes. Well, she was a stronger woman than her mother had been. He'd find that out soon enough.

After her shower, she dried her hair and used Spider's brush to twist it back into the severe coil that she'd worn for years. She brushed her teeth with the new toothbrush she'd found and bemoaned the lack of even the few cosmetics she ordinarily used. Or clean undergarments.

There was a knock on the door and she almost jumped out of her skin. "Yes?"

"It's me. I got your clothes from the cleaners. Your panty hose were pretty well shot, so I picked up some more at the drugstore. I got some other stuff you might want, too."

"Thank you," she said softly as she leaned her head against the door. Dear Lord, it hadn't even occurred to her that a perfect stranger had done something so intimate as pull off her stockings. The last thing she remembered was gulping a double shot of bourbon that Spider had pressed into her hand.

"If you'll toss your underwear out, I'll stick it in the washer and drier for you."

So much for modesty. She looked at the French silk items lying on the hamper and was caught between laughing and crying. They would never survive a washing machine. "Uh . . . no, thank you. I'll do them later at Vicki's."

She could almost see him shrug. "I'll leave your stuff on the bed."

When she was sure he was gone, Anne peeked out the bathroom door. Finding the room empty, she went to the bed. Her cream-colored wool slacks and beige silk blouse lay on hangers beside a paper bag. The sack contained a pair of panty hose in a plastic egg, spray deodorant in a blue can with flowers, a bottle of hand lotion, and a tube of pink lipstick.

She sat down on the side of the bed and hugged the lumpy brown sack to her like a treasure. Never had she been given a more thoughtful or cherished gift. If she ever got out of this mess, she would never, never take anything for granted again.

Anne sat in Spider's office, which was located next to his bedroom. A large executive desk of finely oiled pecan was littered with piles of papers, and peanut shells spilled out of an overflowing ashtray. Scores of framed photographs hung on the walls. A set of snow tires occupied one corner, and an inflatable mattress leaned in another. Below a one-way mirror with a view of the shop, four mismatched filing cabinets lined one wall, their tops covered with silver trophies. Amid the dusty trophies were a magnificent Erté bronze, an intricately carved jade censer, and a stuffed monkey. She shook her head at the strange assortment and picked up the phone to call Vicki.

"This is Victoria Chase. I'm sorry—"

Anne slammed down the phone.

Spider stuck his head in the door. "Something wrong, sugar?"

"I got that blasted recording again! I thought surely she would be home by now."

"Maybe she screens her calls before she answers."

Anne brightened for a moment, then frowned. "And maybe she's out of town. I don't dare leave my name or a message on a tape."

"Anne, aren't you being a little paranoid?"

She laughed bitterly. "You don't know Preston. He's capable of anything. You can't imagine what I've been through the past two weeks. It's a miracle I'm still alive."

Spider pulled up a chair beside her. "Why don't you tell me about it?"

His blue eyes seemed so sympathetic that she was tempted to spill the whole story to him. She'd have liked to tell him about coming home from Europe just as Preston's poker game with two senators, a Cabinet memeber, a general, and a director of the FBI was breaking up. She'd been away for a few months after her mother's death, to rest and ostensibly take time to consider Preston's proposal of marriage—although she'd never seriously entertained such a notion. When she returned, she'd noticed several cars leaving.

Thinking him alone, she'd gone to the door of Preston's study and overheard a conversation that when she thought of it still sent chills over her. It would be a relief to share her burden with someone, but she didn't dare. If she couldn't trust the police, how could she trust a stranger?

Even though Spider had been kind to her, she knew how the allure of money could affect people. And though she found herself strangely attracted to his rough, dark good looks, she knew nothing of his character. If the price were right he might betray her without hesitation. Allowing blue eyes and a coarse sort of charm to negate her good sense would be the height of foolishness.

She shook her head. "I can't."

He looked at her for a moment, then reached for the phone. "Who is this Vicki? Tell me something about her."

Anne tensed. "Why do you want to know?"

"Don't be so skittish, sugar. If I'm going to call her and leave a message, it has to sound legit."

Still suspicious of his motives, she worried her pearls while she considered her options. At that moment, there were none. "She's . . . an attorney."

"She have a brother?"

Anne was puzzled by his question, but she nodded. "One older, one younger. And a younger sister."

"Tell me about her older brother."

"His name is Bob—Robert Chase—and he's president of an insurance company in Dallas."

He asked for Vicki's number, then punched it in. After a moment he said, "Vicki, this is Bill Webb. Your brother Bob asked me to contact you

about some legal business I have in Houston. Give
me a call when you get in. It's important that I
talk with you as soon as possible." He gave his
number, hung up, and grinned. "That ought to
do it."

"I seem to be thanking you all the time." She
smiled. "Is your name really Bill?"

"Yep. William Andrew Webb. But nobody's called
me anything but Spider since I was in high school."

"Why were you called Spider?"

"I guess it's a logical nickname for somebody
named Webb, but mostly it stuck from the years I
played tight end. They said I caught the ball like a
fly in a spiderweb."

"Tight end? Isn't that some sort of position in
football?"

One big hand slapped his chest. "You've wounded
my ego." He feigned an aggrieved look. "Yes, a
tight end is a position in football. Once upon a
time I was hot stuff in the pros. I played with the
Raiders for eight years before I was traded to the
Oilers. I only played in Houston for a year before
my knee got banged up."

For the first time in her life, Anne was embarrassed that she knew nothing about football. It
was obviously an important part of Spider's past,
but she couldn't even make an intelligent response.
She laid her hand on his arm.

"I'm sorry about your injury."

He patted her hand. "Me too. Me too. It ended a
lot of things for me."

The feel of his hand on hers sent a peculiar
ripple of warm prickles up her arm. Trying to

make the gesture casual, she extricated her hand. "You can't play football anymore?"

"There's not much of a market for a pass receiver who can't run."

Although he cloaked his answer with a self-derisive laugh, Anne felt the pain of his words, and she longed to comfort him. With a little coaxing, he told her about his career as a professional football player and showed her the various pictures on the walls of him with celebrities and former teammates. There was pride in his blue eyes when he told her about being the Raiders' first-round draft selection and about winning the Super Bowl.

"I'm impressed," she told him honestly.

He tried to hide a grin as he picked up the jade censer from atop the cluttered file cabinet and lifted the lid. "Jelly bean?" he said, offering the delicately carved container to her. She looked horrified, and he frowned. "You have something against jelly beans?"

She took a red one to keep from offending him, then said quietly, "Do you know the value of that piece?"

"Sure." He set it back on the filing cabinet. "Three hundred and thirty bucks. And I'm stuck with it because the owner didn't get it out of hock."

"It's worth at least fifty times that much."

Spider's brows shot up. "You're kidding."

"And this particular Erté—" she touched the fanciful gown of the bronze statuette "—would easily bring ten thousand dollars at a gallery."

He stuck his hands under his armpits and rocked back on his heels. "Well, I'll be damned. Are you sure?"

"Positive. I have a master's degree in art history, and I—" She stopped herself before she revealed that she owned a gallery in Washington and had sold similar items. "You didn't know?"

He shook his head. "The art stuff was always Pinky's department."

"Pinky?"

"Charles Pinkham. He was my partner. He used to be my butler, but that's another story." Spider grinned. "He sold out to me last August and went back to England."

In a terrible breach of good manners, her eyes widened. "*You* had a butler?" Then, horrified by her tactless words, she dropped her gaze. "Please, forgive me. It's certainly none of my affair."

"Hell, darlin', it's no secret. It made the front page of all the grocery-store tabloids. Yeah, I had a butler and a swimming pool and a six-bedroom house on the golf course. I drove a Ferrari and had a little ranch up near Brenham. I had a ton of blue-chip stocks and money to burn. The whole nine yards."

Anne couldn't help asking. "What happened?"

"I spent six weeks in the hospital. The day I was released, I came hobbling home on crutches and with a big cast on my leg to find that my wife and my business manager had cleaned me out. They'd liquidated everything and lit out together. All that was left in the house—which was only leased, I found out later—were my football trophies, the divorce papers, and Pinky."

She put her hand on his arm. "How terrible for you. I'm so sorry."

He shrugged. "It's water under the bridge."

"Couldn't you recover your property?"

"I could if I could find them. They left the country. They're living in high cotton somewhere in Europe or South America. I wouldn't have a plugged nickel if it hadn't of been for Pinky and this place. My business manager had loaned a wad of my money to his brother-in-law to open a pawnshop. He was six months behind in his payments, so I kicked him out and Pinky and I took over. I've done okay."

Anne felt a catch in her throat. "It hurts when people you trust betray you."

"Yes it does, sugar. Yes it does. But you can't let it turn you sour. There are some nice people mixed in with the slimeballs out there."

Their conversation flowed so easily that before she realized it, it was noon. Spider sent one of the men who worked for him to the deli for sandwiches and coleslaw. By midafternoon, Vicki still hadn't phoned, and Anne began to grow anxious.

"Come on. Let's go to her place and check with the neighbors."

Relieved at his suggestion, she agreed and picked up the briefcase she'd left under his desk. Spider donned his black jacket and went into one of the storerooms. He came back with a suede coat, deep taupe and in a Western cut, with long fringe at the shoulders and down the sleeves. Though it was obviously expensive, Anne would never before have considered wearing such an outlandish thing.

"I think the cold front has moved through, but it's still a little chilly out. This ought to be about your size," he said, holding it out for her to put on. "A River Oaks lady hocked it after the rodeo last year, and I haven't seen her since."

It was a perfect fit. Running her fingers over the buttery-soft leather and inhaling the distinctive smell of fine suede, she looked up at Spider, who seemed to be waiting for her reaction like a small boy seeking approval. She gave him a smile. "Thank you. It's lovely. I'll take good care of it."

He turned up the collar and his hands lingered on her lapels. For several seconds he simply stood there, silent and looking into her face with black-lashed eyes as blue and haunting as a South Sea lagoon. His gaze dropped to her lips, and they parted slightly, as if to a silent command. A warm fluttering stirred in her stomach. Every feminine instinct she possessed told her that he wanted to kiss her. She swayed toward him, pulled by an incomprehensible magnetism, then stopped as alarm spread over her.

Spider gave a little shake of his head and, as if nothing had passed between them, grabbed her arm and propelled her out the back way. He led her to a big truck, shiny black and liberally decorated with chrome.

When he opened the door, the cab looked a million miles off the ground, and, dismayed, she turned to him, then resolutely looked back at the seat.

He looked amused as she awkwardly scrambled up into the cab. "Where to?" he asked when he got behind the wheel.

She gave him Vicki's address and hoped her friend would be home. Being around Spider Webb was disconcerting. Very disconcerting.

In less than five minutes, they pulled to a stop on a winding street lined with distinctive town houses. When she reached for the door handle, Spider stopped her.

"You stay in the truck, Anne. Let me check this out."

Anne watched as he went through the courtyard and knocked on the door. After what seemed like an eternity, he knocked again. She twirled the fringe of her jacket around her finger as she waited. He walked away from the door and shrugged at her, then went to the next house and knocked. The door opened and he talked to someone for a few minutes.

As he returned to the truck, Spider's face was unreadable, and she twirled the fringe faster. When he was settled back in the truck he turned to her, and his eyes seemed troubled.

"Sugar, I've got some bad news."

Three

When he hesitated, Anne's heart flew to her throat. Had Preston's thugs done something to her friend? Dear Lord, surely not. Surely he hadn't recalled her connection to VIcki. She balled her hands into fists so tightly that her nails bit into the flesh of her palms.

"Has she been hurt?"

He shook his head. "No, nothing like that."

Anne breathed a relieved sigh. Vicki was safe. There was still hope. "Where is she?"

"Sugar, your friend's gone on a cruise for a month, and there's no way to contact her. She left last week."

"Oh, no." Try as she might, Anne couldn't prevent the tears that sprang to her eyes. "What am I going to do?" She felt as if her heart were being ripped from her chest. "I was counting on Vicki. I don't have any money. I don't have a place to live. I can't go home. What am I going to do?"

"Aw, darlin', don't cry." He pulled her close and wound his strong arms around her. "You can stay with me."

Taken aback by his proposition, she sobered and pushed away. "I can't stay with you!"

"Then what will you do? Is there somebody else you can stay with? Family? Friends?"

She shook her head. "I'll . . . I'll find an apartment and get a job."

"Sugar, you don't have any money. To get a decent apartment, you'll have to have identification and money enough for a deposit and the first and last month's rent. You'll need clothes and food and money for utilities. And you don't have a fork or a stick of furniture."

Anne felt despair closing in on her again, and she closed her eyes and tried to think. An idea came to her and her eyes flew open. "You said you'd buy my watch."

"Yeah, I'll buy it, but I can't give you what it's worth. It might cover setting you up in an apartment, but what about clothes and food? And what about transportation? You don't have a driver's license or a social security card. Nobody's going to give you a job without identification or references."

No, she dare not give references. Reality settled on her shoulders like a hundred-pound weight, and she dropped her head back against the seat. She had reached the end of the road. She had exhausted her meager list of friends and acquaintances, and Preston had always been one step ahead of her in any case.

"Except me," Spider said.

"Pardon?"

"I'll give you a job. Since Pinky's been gone, you can see what kind of mess things have gotten in, and you seem to know about the arty stuff. I need somebody to organize and appraise it, maybe help me sell off some of the pieces. Think you could handle the job?"

Anne brightened. "Certainly I could. Do I have the job?"

"You've got it."

He squeezed her hand, and his gaze ranged over her face with a look that instinctively put her on guard. More than a friendly interest radiated from the blue depths of his eyes, and her heart reacted with an increased tempo. She was intensely aware of his rugged, masculine appeal. A pulsating aura of sensuality surrounded him, drifted over her, and insinuated itself in the marrow of her bones.

It excited her.

Jolted by the realization, she forced herself to look away. She couldn't allow herself even to fantasize getting involved with someone like him. Such an idea was madness.

"Would you help me find a place to live until Vicki gets home?"

"You've got a place to live. With me."

"But I can't live with you."

"Why not?"

Visions of him stretched out beside her on red satin sheets stampeded through her mind. Horrified at the errant turn of her thoughts, she burst out, "Well . . . well, I just don't *do* that sort of thing."

One corner of his full mouth curved upward. "Sugar, I didn't mean you had to sleep in my bed. I don't mess with married women. You're safe with me."

"But I'm—" She clamped her mouth shut.

He gave her a knowing smile. "You're not really divorced, are you?"

She shook her head. Neither was she married, but perhaps it was wise to indulge in the pretense for the time being. She needed the shield. As long as he assumed she wasn't free, he would keep his distance. Spider didn't "mess" with married women as he so delicately put it

"We'll clean out one of the storage rooms and make a place for you. It may not be a suite at the Royal Fox, but it's free."

At the mention of the Royal Fox Hotel, panic seized her. Did he suspect her connection with the elite chain? She searched his face for any sign of duplicity. His gaze was steady, his expression guileless. No, he couldn't know. Her family had always been low-key and had avoided publicity of any kind. The strange turn of events she'd experienced had made her suspicious of everyone.

"Thank you." She smiled.

"Don't mention it. Let's stop and buy you a nightgown. I have to be back to relieve Molly and Fred by six."

"Who are Molly and Fred?"

"You didn't meet them, did you? They work for me. Fred and another fellow named Boots work full-time and Molly comes in part-time. She's going to college. I'll get Molly to take you shopping for some clothes Monday."

"I wouldn't want to impose."

"Impose?" He shot her an amused look. "Molly will get a kick out of it. She's majoring in fashion."

When they pulled into a vacant space near the entrance of a gigantic store and Anne saw the crowd of shoppers inside, tension begin to tighten her muscles. A man getting into a red car nosed against the truck stared at them for a long time, and her heart almost stopped. She averted her face, slunk down in the seat, and automatically grabbed for the handle of the briefcase sitting between her feet.

"Sugar, what's the matter? You're as white as a sheet."

"That man is staring at us."

"What man?"

"The man in the red car in front of us. What if he recognized me?"

Spider frowned. She was wound tighter than a three-dollar watch. Was Anne so scared that she was jumping at her own shadow, or had he gotten tied up with a crazy lady? He looked up to see a middle-aged man in a green Windbreaker giving them the once-over.

"Wait here." Spider climbed out of the black Silverado and sauntered over to the man. "Something wrong, partner?"

The man grinned and stuck out his hand. "You're Spider Webb, aren't you? Damn, I thought that was you. I'm Ed Ehrlich. The Oilers sure have missed having you in the lineup. Any chance you'll be back?"

Spider laughed and shook Ed's hand. "Not much chance." He talked with the man for a couple of minutes, then walked back to the truck and opened Anne's door. "Nothing to worry about, sugar. He recognized me, not you. He's a football fan."

He could see relief wash over her and color return to her delicate face. It ticked him off to know that her idiot of a husband had her so spooked that she almost freaked out when somebody just looked at her. She didn't deserve to have to hide out like an escaped convict.

His gaze dropped to her hands, which were still clutching the handle of her eel-skin briefcase. She'd been hauling that satchel around with her all day. His eyes narrowed. What did she have in there?

"How could he have recognized you, sugar? You're a long way from home."

"Yes, but you don't know my . . . you don't know him. One slip and he'll find me. That robber last night—" she bit her lip "—if he abandoned my car somewhere and it was found, Preston would know I'm in Houston. And my purse. If he took the money and threw the purse away . . . my identification . . ."

He took one of her hands in his. It was cold as an icicle. "Darlin,' don't worry about the car being found. I'd bet my last dime it went to a chop shop, got painted black, and is halfway to California by now. And your purse and ID are at the bottom of some dumpster with a ton of coffee grounds, chicken bones, and beer cans on top."

"Do you really think so?"

He smiled. "Trust me. I grew up around here, and I know all about the kind of scum that ripped you off last night. I know the way they operate. The scratch that hophead could make off a Jag could keep him high for a long time. He wouldn't pass up a sweet deal like that one."

Anne's eyes widened. "He was on drugs?"

"Higher than a kite. Come on. Let's go get you a nightgown." When she hesitated, he reached into the glove compartment, pulled out a pair of mirrored sunglasses, and perched them on her cute little nose. He also pulled out a billed cap endorsing a beer company. He beat the black cap on his thigh a couple of times and stuck it on her head. "There," he said with a grin, "now even your grandmother wouldn't recognize you."

She laughed and took the hand he offered to help her out of the truck. He noticed that she seemed more relaxed as they walked toward the store. He also noticed that she lugged the briefcase with her.

With the help of a clerk, they started toward the lingerie section of the huge store. As they wound their way around gigantic stacks of hair spray and displays of corn chips, Anne remarked, "This is an interesting place. They certainly have everything in the world here, don't they?"

He grinned down at the slender woman trotting beside him and slowed his stride. "Just about."

While Anne looked through a stack of nightgowns, Spider plucked a slinky red one from a rack. She'd look sexy as hell in it, with the lace cups hugging her breasts and the tiny straps show-ing off her soft skin. Slit up one side and sheer enough to tease the treasure it covered, it was a gown that begged a man to take it off. Just think-ing about her dressed in it made desire curl in his stomach. "How about this one?" he asked, hold-ing it up and fanning out the transparent skirt.

She gave him a quelling glance over the top of the aviator glasses, which had slipped to the tip of her nose. "How about this one instead?" She shook out a flannel granny gown and held the long white garment up to herself.

She was married, Spider reminded himself. *Married.* "Yeah, maybe that one would be better. Why don't you get another one in blue? Blue's my favorite color."

"I need a few other things. Is that a problem?"

He smiled at her. "Don't worry about paying for it. We'll call it an advance on your salary."

"Thank you," she said gratefully. While she picked out some underwear he gathered up a blue fleece robe and some terry-cloth slippers. While she was looking at bras, he wandered over to a rack of jeans. Soft and comfortable-looking, they were a designer brand that even he recognized. He selected a couple and took them to her.

"Why don't you try these on?" he asked.

"Do we have time?"

"Sure. What size shoes do you wear?"

"Six and a half, narrow. But I have shoes."

They both looked down at the high-heeled boots she wore. "I know you do, sugar. And they're just as cute as they can be, but wearing those things all the time must be murder on your feet. I saw some sneakers over there. Good price. I'll get you some."

By the time they were ready to check out, Spider was pushing a basket piled high with gowns, robe, slippers, underwear, jeans, shirts, sweaters —he noticed she'd selected a blue one—shoes, socks, a hairbrush, a purse, and cosmetics. He'd even tossed in a few items of his own. Some razor blades and a bag of Chee-tos. And a sack of peppermints. She'd said she liked peppermints better than jelly beans.

As they waited in line at the checkout with their overflowing basket, he cocked an eyebrow at Anne, who looked extremely pleased with herself. "Think this will do you till Monday?"

She looked stricken. "Is it too much?"

"Nah, I was kidding." He laughed and pushed the sunglasses up on her nose. "We're going to have to see about getting you a better disguise. I'll give a friend of mine a call in the morning. She's good at that sort of thing. Let's get back to the Parlor before Fred and Molly send out the posse."

As they drove back to the pawnshop with their purchases piled on the seat between them, Anne was thanking the powers that be for finding Spider. He'd been a lifesaver—literally. Of course, if she hadn't gone to hock her watch, she'd still have her car. She could have sold it for enough to live on for a long time. But she *had* gone to the pawnshop, and her car *had* been stolen, and there was no use in dwelling on what might have been. Considering Preston's power and influence, she'd been lucky so far.

It was pure luck that she'd overheard her stepbrother's conversation with Bradley Stanfield, a deputy director of the FBI. She'd gone to her stepbrother's study to tell him that she had returned from her trip, thinking that since he had guests she'd wait until the next morning to gently refuse his kind proposal of marriage. Ironically, she'd been concerned about hurting his feelings.

The door had been slightly ajar, and she'd just raised her hand to knock when a man's voice shouted, "Damn it, Pres! You can't ask me to do this!"

"I can, and I will," her stepbrother had answered calmly. "Need I remind you, Bradley, that it was *I* who secured your appointment as deputy director? Need I remind you of the extremely sensitive file in my safe?"

"But the man's reputation will be ruined." Bradley's argument had sounded merely perfunctory.

"Perhaps, but I want his Senate seat. Do it."

Shocked at what she'd overheard, Anne had stood frozen outside the door.

"It's going to take a lot of money."

"I have access to millions," Preston had replied.

"That was while the old lady was alive. The daughter may be different."

"I've asked Anne to become my wife. In addition to her fortune, her Foxworth-Jennings blue blood will be an asset to me in my political climb. She's a gracious hostess and malleable. As long as she has her charge accounts and her little gallery to dabble in a couple of days a week, she'll be happy. I'll still control the estate."

"What if she won't marry you?"

"Then we'll have to arrange a little accident. If she dies without heirs, everything comes to me."

When her shock had faded, Anne's first impulse had been to run. And run she had. But she'd kept her wits enough to take the documents in the briefcase before she'd escaped from her own house.

Thoughts of that night brought back all the feelings of horror, disbelief, and anger she'd experienced. The horror and disbelief had diminished. Anger remained. And fear. She'd be lying if she said she wasn't afraid of Preston. She didn't underestimate him; he was a formidable enemy. But she was determined to see him exposed and locked away for his treachery.

She touched the briefcase that sat between her feet. Preston knew that she had the files. And she knew he would never stop looking for her. He still had access to almost unlimited resources, She hoped he would never think to look for her in a pawnshop in Houston.

Anne stood staring at the water bed Spider and Boots, a lanky, red-haired man who worked for Spider, had assembled earlier that evening. Set in a frame of dark knotty pine, it was covered with sheets in a wild print of stalking tigers and panthers peeking through fronds of jungle foliage. It was a far cry from the cherry four-poster and rose silk coverlet in her room at home.

"What do you think?" Spider stepped through the doorway of the storeroom across from his office.

"It's . . . fine. I appreciate your and Boots doing this. It was very nice of him to help."

"No problem. He was glad to do it. Even though," he said, giving her a wicked wink, "he didn't understand why we needed two beds."

Her breath caught and a flush of heat crept up her neck. She tried to smile at his teasing, but her mouth felt frozen. With him standing so close in the crowded area, the small room seemed to shrink to minuscule proportions.

"We'll get some more of this stuff cleared out tomorrow," he said, gesturing toward the stacks of boxes and disordered assortment of pawned merchandise piled up and shoved against the walls. There was barely enough room to walk around the bed.

He bent over the mattress and tested it with one large, splayed hand. His action set the surface rocking. As if mesmerized, Anne watched the slow, rippling undulations, blatantly suggestive and extremely disconcerting. Still she stared, spellbound by the seductive movement of tropical foliage and predatory animals.

"I don't think it has any leaks. And the sheets are clean." He handed her the fur throw from his bed, and she dragged her gaze from the quivering jungle. "In case your granny gown doesn't keep you warm enough," he told her in a low, rumbling voice as he stroked the dark nap of the plush bundle she held.

Light caught the cutlass hanging from his ear and struck blue fire in his eyes as she looked up at him. A growing awareness of his nearness crawled across her skin and burrowed into the pit of her stomach. Even with dusty, musty odors permeating the storeroom, she could pick up his distinctive warm scent. Citrus and sandalwood and virile male.

It was intoxicating. Magnetic. Inexplicably titillating. Spider Webb exuded a masculine charisma that was thick enough to be cut in wedges and served up like Black Forest cake.

Several years ago, her neighbor Betsy Carmichael had braved the disapproval of her friends and family to run off with a rough-cut type from Oregon.

"He may not have prep-school polish or own a suit, but he's *all* man," she had overheard Betsy say to one of her friends at the country club. "And he makes me feel *all* woman. Honey, I don't know what he's got, but it's dynamite."

For the first time, she understood what Betsy was talking about. Anne could almost hear the hiss of a lighted fuse. She stepped back and bumped into a sewing machine. "But I don't want to take your cover."

He reached out and drew the length of his index finger down the side of her cheek. His sensual lips parted slowly, then curved upward just as slowly. "No problem. I'm hot-natured."

The room shrank even smaller.

Spider threw the wet towel on the floor and sprawled across his bed. Cold showers were vastly overrated. It hadn't helped a damned bit. Every inch of his bare, damp body had turned to an erogenous zone.

An hour later, he lay there. Wide awake. Restless, miserable. She was married, he told himself for the hundredth time. And way out of his league. And with troubles he didn't need.

His body didn't seem to care. It was sending his brain signals that set off erotic visions that made his body ache even worse. It was an endless cycle that had kept him tossing and turning and swearing at himself.

Flopping over on his side, he punched his pillow and willed himself to go to sleep. His hand stroked the smooth satin sheet, and he thought about the smoothness of her skin and how her breasts would feel cupped in his hands. What would they taste like? His tongue tingled and he rubbed it over the roof of his mouth.

He turned onto his stomach, but all he could think about was her under him with those long legs clamped around his waist. He could imagine her big brown eyes looking up at him and her sweet mouth calling his name. He muttered another oath and rolled onto his back. What was it about Anne? Maybe it was her softness, her shy vulnerability.

Damn! And maybe it was because he'd been without a woman too long. He tried to get his mind on other things. He dredged up old football games, plays he'd run, passes he'd caught.

Finally, he drifted off.

A raucous ringing ripped through the building

and jerked him awake. He sat straight up in bed as a streak of white flew through the room and pounced on him in a tangled flurry of flailing arms and legs. Something hard slammed against the bridge of his nose.

Cursing, he flung his assailant aside, straddled the wiggling mass he held pinned against the bed, and drew back his fist.

"Spider!" a feminine voice whispered. "It's me. Anne."

He sat back on his heels. "I nearly creamed you."

"What's that noise?" She sounded frantic.

"The burglar alarm. You stay here."

He reached for the shotgun under his bed and stole across the room, pumping a shell into the barrel as he went. At the door he paused to listen. A soft body collided with his backside, and something banged against the side of his leg.

"I told you to stay put," he hissed.

"I'm coming with you. I'm not staying by myself. Where you go, I go."

Something clipped him on the back of the knee. "What are you carrying?"

"My briefcase."

"Leave the damned thing here."

"Where I go, it goes."

He rolled his eyes. "Well, stay close and stay down," he whispered.

As the strident alarm continued to ring, Turk screamed, "Stop, thief! Put 'em up! I've got you covered!"

Hugging the wall along the hallway, they eased

into Spider's office and closed the door. Anne stuck to him like a grass stain.

Night-lights were on in the shop, and he peered through the one-way mirror, looking for signs of movement. Everything looked quiet. He could feel Anne's breath on his shoulder and her heart beating against his back. One of her arms circled his torso with a death grip, and he looked back at her as she peeked over the edge of his shoulder. She looked scared to death.

"Did somebody break in?" she asked.

"I don't think so. This place is as hard to crack as Fort Knox."

"Then why did the alarm go off?"

He shrugged.

The phone rang. Anne jumped and let out a squeak. "It's okay, darlin'." He patted her hand and reached for the phone. "Spider," he answered. He listened to the caller for a moment. "Right," he said and hung up.

"It's okay. Nothing to be worried about." He laid the shotgun on the desk, gathered Anne into his arms, and held her close against him. She was so close, he could feel her heart hammering in her chest. "That was the security company. It was a false alarm. They had a problem on their end."

"Thank God." She relaxed against him.

He held her a moment longer, her head nestled on his chest, and stroked her back. It felt good to hold her. Everything about her was so sweet and so soft. Even her bones felt delicate and fragile. "Are you all right?"

"Yes," she murmured.

He held her by the upper arms and pushed her back until he could see her face. "Sure?"

She heaved a big sigh and nodded her head.

"Good. I told you I would take care of you." He ached to kiss her, to growl and cover her mouth with the hunger gnawing within him, but he wasn't that unprincipled. He allowed himself only a quick, brotherly peck on her lips. "You stay here while I reset the alarm."

When he started out the door, he heard a gasp and he spun around.

"Spider!" Her eyes were wide. "You're naked!"

He looked down at himself, then back up at her. He grinned and shrugged. "Yeah."

"And your nose is bleeding."

He made a swipe with his forearm and saw she was right. "That damned thing you're carrying is a lethal weapon. What have you got in there that's so important?"

She didn't answer. She only stood there with her mouth puckered up, looking like an angel in her long white gown, clutching the satchel to her breasts like a baby, and trying not to stare at him. At that moment, he wanted nothing more than to throw her over his shoulder, haul her to his bed, and spend the rest of the night making slow, sweet love to her.

Married. She was married. On the other hand, her husband was a lowlife and she's scared to death of him, he tried to argue with his conscience. But his conscience won. Married was married.

"I'm going to reset the alarm and put on some pants. Then we're going to talk. I need some answers, and we'll start with what's in that briefcase."

Four

On Sunday morning, Anne and Trish Powell, a friend of Spider's, were the sole occupants in the chic hair salon on San Felipe. Only the sound of their voices disturbed the quiet of the large room, done in mauves and dusky blues and scented with the lingering potpourri of feminine pampering. Anne sat at one of the six work stations with gilt-framed mirrors that surrounded a central seating area outlined by a Persian rug and silk settees in a Louis XV style. A crystal chandelier shone down on a glass coffee table with current copies of fashion magazines and an arrangement of rubrum lilies and chrysanthemums, adding warmth to the elegant ambience.

For the first time since her frantic flight from home, Anne felt a measure of comfort in her environment, less estranged from the world she'd always known. She let the familiar scents and self-indulgent rituals soothe her until her fear seemed very far away. Relaxed, she sat at one of the stations, a mauve cape over her shoulders and her hair in hot rollers. While pink polish dried on her nails, she held her face up for Trish to smooth on a light foundation.

"I'm sorry to trouble you on your day off," Anne said to the friendly woman who had been chattering as if they had known one another for years, "but I feel absolutely, wonderfully decadent."

The exotic, dark-eyed stylist smiled. "We all need a bit of pampering now and then. There's nothing like a new hairdo and a few pots of paint to make us not only look different but feel different. Stronger somehow, ready to tackle the tigers out there. And, believe me, it's no trouble. I owe Spider Webb a lot more than I can ever repay. He helped me when I needed it. It's thanks to him that I own this shop—or half of it. Spider owns the other half."

Anne was surprised. "He didn't tell me that."

Trish laughed. "I'm not surprised. For all his macho swagger, Spider has insides like a Twinkie. He's a good man. I'd trust him with my life. Close your eyes."

When she complied so that Trish could brush on eye shadow, Anne asked, "Have you known him long?"

"We grew up together, but I hadn't seen him since high school until a couple of years ago. I was in a pretty tough spot, a worthless husband and three kids to support. I went to Spider for a loan and before I knew it, we were partners. I've always been a pretty good hairdresser; I just needed a break, and Spider provided it. The business did well right from the beginning. We've developed a very loyal and exclusive clientele. And thank heaven for it. With the income from the salon, I was able to divorce that creep."

Anne opened her eyes. "What did Spider tell you about me?"

Trish dusted Anne's cheeks with blush. "Not much." She added mascara and sat back to study her handiwork. "Just that you were running from an abusive husband and needed a disguise to make you feel safe." With an empathetic smile, Trish looked into Anne's face and patted her hand. "I know the feeling. I've been there."

Guilt twisted Anne's insides. She hated to deceive this kind woman who was giving up a Sunday morning with her children to help a stranger, but she forced herself to smile and say only, "Thank you, Trish."

"No problem. We all need a helping hand now and then. Let's put on your lipstick, and then we'll brush out your hair. I think you're going to be pleasantly surprised."

In a few minutes, Trish turned the chair to face the mirror and said, "Ta-dah!"

Anne stared at the reflection of a glamorous stranger. "It that *me*?"

Trish laughed. "No other. Like it?"

She turned her head from side to side and studied the new look. Gone was the sleek brown topknot. Her hair was now ash blond with lighter blond highlights and cut in a free-swinging style.

Just shy of shoulder length, smooth full waves and a fringe of wispy bangs framed her face. With the new hairdo and makeup, her eyes looked different, her cheekbones more pronounced.

"I love it. I can't believe how different I look." Anne shook her head and laughed. "And how much freer I feel. Trish, it's delightful!"

The stylist grinned. "And it won't be hard to care for." She gave Anne instructions on how to maintain the style and how to apply her new makeup. She also insisted that Anne take along several sample sizes of the cosmetics she'd used.

"Trish, how can I thank you—"

"Don't worry about it. You're a friend of Spider's. And I hope now a friend of mine. You can return the favor sometime."

"Thanks." Anne took the tall woman's hand and gave it a squeeze. "I can always use a friend."

Instead of calling Spider to pick her up, Trish insisted on dropping Anne off at the Pawn Parlor. Anne waved good-bye as they made a promise to get together in a few days. Feeling revitalized and almost giddy with her new image, she buzzed and stood waiting, briefcase in hand, for the door to open.

"Step into my parlor, sweet thing," Turk's mellow voice said as she walked in.

Anne gave a little laugh, bowed to the myna, and said, "Thank you. I will." Still smiling, she strolled toward the back display case, where Spider was working.

He glanced up and did a classic double take. "Anne?"

She laughed and did a slow turn. "Like it?"

A broad grin spread over his face and a thick brow lifted. "Turn around again."

As she did, Spider could feel his temperature rising. It was as if some look-but-don't-touch part of her had been left on the floor of Trish's shop with her hair. While she was still a classy lady, no doubt about it, the uptown, uptight look had mellowed. She seemed looser, more open, like she'd shed a protective shell. Her movements were sassier; her eyes larger, browner, and twinkling.

He hadn't realized earlier just how good the jeans and blue sweater looked on her. But he realized it now. It had been hard to keep his mind off her sweet little curves before. He had a hunch that his days and nights—especially the nights—were going to be tougher than ever.

"Well?" she asked.

He let out a wolf whistle. "Dynamite! I didn't think gorgeous could be improved upon, but you're sensational. I almost didn't recognize you."

She stuck out her bottom lip. "I'm not sure if that's a compliment."

He rubbed a splayed hand over the gray Raiders logo on the chest of his black sweatshirt. "I get the feeling I'm in one of those situations where I'm damned if I do and damned if I don't. Let me try it again."

With a mischievous smile she stood and waited, as if she were determined not to help him out of his predicament.

He cleared his throat. "You're gorgeous. You've

always been gorgeous. Now you're just gorgeous in a different way." He grinned. "How's that?"

"You wiggled out of it quite nicely. I like your friend Trish. And she's very good."

"Yeah. And I really think your new look should fool most people. Do you feel better?"

She nodded.

"Good. You about ready for lunch?"

"Starved."

"Hey, Fred!" A hefty man with thinning brown hair and a gap between his front teeth ambled in from one of the back rooms, and Spider said, "Molly will be here in a few minutes. Anne and I are going out for a bite. Beep me if you need anything."

As they started out the front, Spider held open the door for a small woman with a mink cape over her black dress. "How are you, Mrs. Bremmer?" he asked the gray-haired lady.

"Fine, Spider, just fine." Her blue eyes twinkling, she looked at Anne, then back at him. She leaned close and whispered, "Lovely girl."

He grinned. "Mrs. Bremmer, this is Anne. She's going to be working here for a while. We were on our way to lunch, but may I help you with something today?"

"Oh, no, Spider. You young people run along. I'm just going to browse a bit."

Anne had selected only a tossed salad from the cafeteria line, but Spider, between smiling and speaking to several people who seemed to know him, filled his tray and insisted on heaping more on hers. By the time they reached the register, there wasn't space left for an extra pat of butter.

"I can't eat all this," she said as they unloaded their trays at a table.

He waved her off. "Eat what you want, and we'll take the rest home and microwave it for supper."

Her eyes widened. "You mean like a doggy bag?"

He grinned. "No, I mean like a people bag. The food's great here, and I do it all the time. So does everybody else—see the Styrofoam boxes on the tea cart? Since this is Boots' day off, we won't be able to go out to eat this evening. I have to hold down the Parlor tonight by myself."

"I'll be happy to help if you'll show me what to do."

"I know you would. Try this fish," he said, sliding a serving of baked haddock in front of her. He cut into a slice of rare roast beef and began eating.

"It's very good," she said after consuming a half-portion with her salad. "You're spending too much on me. I'm going to have to start earning my keep. When may I begin work?"

He started to say something, then paused. "We can look around this afternoon, and you can decide what needs to be done."

"I'll need some books from the library to—" She dropped her head and heaved an exasperated sigh.

Frowning, Spider reached for her hand across the table. "What's wrong, darlin'?"

"I can't even get a library card."

"Don't you worry about that. We'll scrape up

some ID for you. The first thing you'll need is a driver's license."

"Don't I need a birth certificate or a passport for that?"

He nodded. "That's no problem. I've got a buddy who can provide you with one."

Her eyebrows shot up. Leaning forward, she whispered, "You mean a *forgery*?"

Shrugging, his lips curved in a you-do-what-you-gotta-do grin. "Any particular name you fancy? Personally, I don't think Smith is a good choice."

Anne had been shocked by the idea of forged identification. The most dishonest thing she had ever done was cheat on a second-grade spelling test, and she'd been so guilt-ridden over the incident that she'd confessed three days later. But common sense reminded her that her present situation called for desperate measures. Being dishonest was better than being dead. Besides, she convinced herself, it wasn't as if she were trying to deceive anyone for nefarious purposes.

"Okay. I'll do it," she declared, as much to herself as to Spider.

By the time they had finished a second glass of iced tea and filled take-home containers with food, they had settled on a new birthday for her and decided that she would use Jennifer Anne Webb and be Spider's cousin.

"I always wanted to be named Jennifer," she told him as they walked through the parking lot.

"And I always wanted a cousin," he said as he helped her into the Silverado. He stowed the briefcase and food on the floor, propped one black-booted foot on the step plate, and hung his elbow on the open door. "I guess we've come a long way if you'll let me carry that satchel of yours, but you still haven't told me what's in it."

Anne nibbled on her lower lip and looked up into bold blue eyes that seemed to peer into places she dared not allow them. She glanced away quickly. "May we discuss it later?"

"That's what you said last night. Don't you know by now you can trust me, sugar?" When she was silent, his mouth curled into a wry grimace. "No, I guess not."

Without another word, he closed the door. Indecision sawed back and forth in her mind as Spider drove to the shop. Instinct prompted her to trust him. Yet, another primitive mechanism whispered that she must not be lulled into revealing her secrets. Her life was too high a stake to gamble on a man she had known only two days. No, she'd wait. She must.

Spider seemed to take in stride her decision to remain silent. That he didn't push said something for his character.

"You're not angry with me?" she ventured after a long silence.

"Nah. I'm not mad. Just curious. I figure you've got some kind of goods on your husband in that thing. Something that could get him in deep grease."

She gasped. "How did you know?"

"Seems logical. He's after you; you're scared witless; you guard that thing like the crown jewels. I figure you've got the goods on him somehow." He glanced over at her with a troubled expression. "Darlin', he's not some honcho with the mob, is he?"

"Why would you ask that?"

"You said he had powerful friends. You're scared of the police. Either you're overreacting or he's tied in with a heck of a network."

"I'm not overreacting," she said fiercely. "And as far as I know Preston doesn't have any connection with the mob."

"Thank God for little miracles."

"Would it matter?"

"You mean would I toss you to the big boys? No, my momma didn't raise me that way. I stick by my friends, but it helps to know the line you're up against." He waited for a response, but she clamped her lips together, determined not to say any more. "Okay, sugar, I figure you'll talk when you're ready. But if I promise nobody will sneak a peek, will you at least lock that thing up in my vault? It's safer than lugging it around with you. I'll even give you the combination."

"I'll think about it."

"Fair enough."

By the time they reached the shop, she had made a decision. The case *would* be safer in the vault than with her. If Spider trusted her enough to provide the combination, she would trust him with the documents. She couldn't live her life being suspicious of everyone.

Once they were inside and had stowed the containers of food in the refrigerator, she drew a deep breath and held out the briefcase. "Here."

He smiled as he took it from her. "I'll take good care of it, darlin'. And instead of putting it in the vault at the back of the shop, I'll put it in the one in my bedroom. Nobody has the combination to that one or knows it's there except me. Come on, I'll show you."

He led her into the room with the big brass bed. Her attention zeroed in on red satin sheets, tangled as if a wrestling match had taken place on the mattress. Before her imagination could take flight, she averted her face and followed him to the corner where the pump organ stood.

He rolled the scarred instrument away from the wall to reveal a large gray safe set in the panel. Black jeans taut across his muscled thighs, he squatted in front of the steel door and dialed the combination, calling out the numbers as he went.

When the door swung open, Anne peered over his shoulder as he rearranged several small bags and stacks of bills. Her eyes widened as she noticed that the currency was in hundreds.

"Don't you believe in banks?" she asked.

"Sure, but I like knowing I've got capital handy. I learned my lesson the last time." He grinned. "I don't trust everybody either." He shoved the briefcase inside, locked the door, and pushed the organ back in place.

When he stood, Anne touched his upper arm. The silver cutlass in his ear gradually stilled as she looked up into his rugged face, shadowed by a faint black stubble. "Thank you for trusting me," she said, "I won't betray you."

"I know you won't."

His hand, large and strong, closed over hers, and his thumb gently stroked the length of her index finger. Sensation swelled from the spot in warm, widening ripples until a shiver chased down her back. Like twin blue fires, his eyes sparked and captured hers, and something in them pulled at her central core. Tiny rings of azure encircling the softly tinted irises seemed to darken and pulsate behind the curve of thick black lashes.

His callused thumb continued its stroking. Her breath caught as tingles spread through her breasts. His eyes were so beautiful, so compelling that she couldn't look away. The muscles beneath her hand hardened and trembled.

Unconsciously, her lips parted and her chin lifted a fraction. His eyes flashed, then shuttered, and his hand drew away.

"I've got to check on something." His tone was gruff, and he turned and strode from the room.

A hollow ache clutched at her chest and a stinging flush crept up her throat. She was mortified by her behavior. And his. She'd almost thrown herself at him. And had been rebuffed.

She looked at the boar's head on the wall. He seemed to be grinning. "I guess I'm not his type."

It was just as well. If he'd kissed her, things could have gotten complicated. Right now she needed a friend more than she needed a lover. Yet—she touched her lips—she couldn't help but wonder how it would have felt.

Business had been slow that evening. They had settled into mismatched easy chairs in the workroom off the rear of the shop, where Spider was watching a colorized World War II movie on television. Just before closing time, Anne glanced up from the magazine she was reading to find him staring at her, his eyes narrowed so that only a sliver of blue shone through his lashes.

Uncomfortable with his scrutiny, she quickly looked back down at the magazine and shifted her position in the chair, drawing her feet under her. After she'd read the same paragraph four times, she glanced up again. He was still staring, his face drawn into a mask so tight that the scar on his cheek stood in bold relief. His gaze was so intense and ominous that fine hairs on her arms rose with a ripple of chill bumps.

Determined not to put herself in the embarrassing position that she had earlier, she said casually, "Is something wrong?"

"No. Nothing's wrong." He turned back to the TV.

Although he'd been the soul of patience showing her around the various rooms where merchandise was stored, explaining their ticketing procedures, and answering questions, something was different. Since their strange encounter in his bedroom, it was as if a subtle, but impenetrable, wall had been erected between them. He had gone from open and friendly to aloof, and his mixed messages were confusing. His behavior was so peculiar that she was beginning to dread the next three weeks of close company. If he didn't want her around, it was time she found out.

"Spider, are you—"

The door to the shop buzzed. He looked relieved as he sprang to his feet. "Customer."

Married, he told himself for the umpteenth time. But Lord she looked so great cuddled up in that chair that he'd almost ground his teeth to the gums to keep from dragging her into his lap and cuddling her up to him. And when she looked at him with those big brown eyes . . . He knew he was acting like a first-class jerk, but he sure as hell couldn't tell her what was the matter with him. What a mess!

He strode into the shop with Anne hot on his heels, glad to see Willie Triner.

"Hey, Willie, how's it going, buddy?" He grabbed the weasel-faced man's hand and pumped it up and down as if they hadn't seen each other for years. The truth was they got together for a beer a couple of times a month. "What can I do for you?"

Looking at Spider as if he'd lost his mind, Willie frowned over the top of his wire-rimmed glasses. "I got the stuff you ordered. You said it was a rush job." His eyes darted to Anne, then back to Spider.

"She's okay, Willie. This is my *cousin* Jennifer Anne Webb."

The man gave a curt nod, pulled a brown envelope from his battered briefcase, and handed it to Spider. "One birth certificate, aged; one social security card; two credit cards." His prominent Adam's apple jiggled up and down as he chuckled. "I used Spider's number on the plastic, ma'am, so they'll pass if anybody checks, but don't run up his account *too* much."

Anne lifted her chin and said, "I wouldn't do that."

Spider threw his arm around her shoulders and hugged her to him. "He was just kiddin', sugar."

She gave an embarrassed little "Oh," and Spider couldn't help but squeeze her again.

"Well, I'll be getting along. The missus and the kids are waiting in the car."

"Thanks, Willie," Spider said. "I owe you one."

"Nah, I haven't caught up with the ones I owe you yet." He gave Anne a nod and left.

When the door closed behind him, Anne said, "He's an interesting little man. I've never met a professional forger before."

Spider grinned down at the bundle of sweet innocence still tucked under his arm. He ought to let her go, but she felt so damned good close to him that he pushed his luck and kept her there. "He's not a professional forger. He owns the biggest string of print shops in town. Hell, he's a deacon in the church."

"Then why? . . ." She seemed bewildered.

"Willie and I go way back. I used to work for him when I was a kid, running errands, sweeping up. Back then, he only owned a one-man shop on the east side. He might have pulled a shady deal or two to keep bread on the table, but he's a good man."

She put her hand on his chest and looked up at him with eyes big enough to swim in. "You have a lot of friends, don't you, Spider?"

When she touched him, he thought his heart was going to rip itself out it was pounding so hard. The flowery smell of her, the soft feel of her had worked itself into his pores. At that moment, he'd have given everything he owned to kiss her.

He tried to tell himself to pull away, but he felt as if the whole Pittsburgh line had piled on top of him. He couldn't move. He ached to taste her, just once.

Anne stood spellbound, fascinated with the contour of his lips, with the line that creased the lower one and divided it into two curves, sensuous and full. How soft, how warm his lips would feel.

His mouth parted slowly, and hers responded in kind. A yearning, deep and unbidden, unfurled within her and beckoned him with ethereal fingers. It swelled and swayed, like the eerie enticement of water plants rippling in gentle currents along the ocean's floor.

His face moved toward hers in maddening gradual descent, as if pulled by the force of longing inside her. His eyes glittered like blue crystals, and as he drew closer, his distinctive scent filled her nostrils. She breathed in, savoring the delicious sensation. Her lids fluttered shut, and her hand pressed and moved across the solid expanse of his chest.

"Oh, *Lord*, darlin'," he groaned, and his mouth captured hers with a consuming power that stole the strength from her bones.

He kissed her with a devouring hunger. Overwhelmed by the intensity of his kiss, she clutched the front of his shirt for support. Growls from his throat reverberated in her mouth as he moved and tasted and laved with his tongue.

Her fingers left the hold on his shirt and threaded through the thick hair curling over the nape of his neck. His other arm snaked around her, pulling her close along his rock-hard length. Whimpering, she strained toward the wonderfully ravenous siege of his lips and tongue.

Suddenly, he went still. His breathing ragged, his chest heaving, he pulled away and spat out a curse. "I've got to lock up." His brows drawn together in a single black slash, he thrust her away and stalked off.

Five

Anne sat at the yellow Formica table in the small kitchen, buttering toast and watching Spider beat eggs as if he held a personal grudge against them. His face was drawn into a fierce scowl, and he looked as if he hadn't slept any better than she had.

Except for one or two grunts, he had said barely a word to her this morning, and he kept his back to her as he worked at the stove. Things couldn't go on like this. She poured coffee into each of their mugs and waited for him to sit down.

When he did, she looked up from the food he'd set in front of her. He sat hunched over, fork poised, studying the heap of scrambled eggs on his plate.

"Spider," she said quietly, "I think it would be better if I found another place to live."

His head flew up, his swarthy scowl even more ferocious. "No!"

She flinched and her fork clattered to her plate.

He let out his favorite expletive of disgust and swiped his hand across his face. "Lord, Anne, I didn't mean to scare you. I wouldn't hurt you for anything in the world. And I'm sorry about last night. Hell, I don't know what got into me. I promised I'd take care of you, told you I didn't mess with married women, and damned if I didn't come on to you like a pumped-up bull."

His hand swiped his face again, sliding over the dark stubble on his chin to rub across his throat as if he'd have liked to choke himself. "I want you to stay here with me so I can protect you. I swear—I'll swear it on a stack of Bibles a mile high—that I won't touch you again if you'll stay."

His face softened, and pale blue eyes implored. It was on the tip of her tongue to tell him that she wasn't married and that she'd wanted the kiss as much as he. But something stopped her. He *had* frightened her. And she had frightened herself. She'd never experienced sexual feelings as potent as those unleashed by his kiss. Jolted to the core of her being, she hadn't known that emotions as intense as those existed. She'd wanted to rip off her clothes and make wild love to him on top of the gun case. She shuddered with the memory. Anne Foxworth Jennings just didn't *do* things like that.

"Sugar?"

She looked up from the paper napkin she'd twisted into a tight blue snake.

"Please stay." He gave her a hangdog look. "Don't you like me?"

"Of course I like you, Spider. You've done so many wonderful things for me, how could I help it? But my life is complicated enough without—"

"Without me hitting on you. I know. I'm sorry about that, sugar. Just as sorry as I can be. If I could take it back, I would. But don't let one slip screw things up. You're a lovely lady, and the truth is, I'm attracted to you. Damned attracted. I'd be lying if I didn't admit it. I just let myself forget for a minute that you're married and don't need anything from me right now but friendship. You don't have anyplace to go, and I'd worry about you out on the streets by yourself. Please stay. I'll give you my word that it won't happen again. You're safe with me."

Anne hesitated. Maybe he did just want to be her friend, but, without even trying, he was the most seductive man she'd ever encountered. A six-foot-four hunk of animal magnetism. Raw sensuality seeped from his pores and invaded the air that she breathed. Even his hair was sexy. At this very moment, her fingers itched to run themselves through the enticing shock, thick and black as sin, curling over his forehead and down his nape. She wanted to rub her cheek against his jaw and feel the rough texture of his stubble against her skin. Her lips ached—

"I promise." He made an X on his chest. "Cross my heart and hope to die." He gave her a slow grin designed to melt steel.

Warmth sparked and smoked low within her. If she stayed, she was courting heartache. This man was too far removed from her world for her to be serious about. If she'd had another option, she would have walked out the door. But her practical nature reminded her that without money, there were no other options. She would have to trust him to keep their relationship platonic. She sighed. "All right. I'll stay."

"Great!" His grin widened, and his eyes grew bright. "Eat up, darlin'. We're going to get your driver's license this morning. I figured you might have a hard time with my pickup, so I'll borrow Fred's Toyota for you to take your test."

He attacked his eggs with gusto, but she only pushed hers around on her plate. Self-reproach crawled in her stomach with a hundred furry feet and made her queasy. It wasn't right to let him keep on believing that she was married, but it was an excellent defense against stampeding hormones. His *and* hers. At two o'clock this morning, after a restless night of tossing and turning, it had taken a great deal of willpower to keep from walking those few steps from her sensuously undulating bed and slipping into one covered with red satin sheets.

Her only salvation was the knowledge that she wasn't cut out for casual affairs. Perhaps she was prim according to today's standards, but recreational sex simply wasn't part of her value system. And she couldn't imagine any other kind of relationship with Spider. She tried to picture an unshaven man in jeans and black leather jacket, a cutlass dangling from his ear, sipping cocktails at an embassy reception in Washington or mingling with patrons at a gallery showing. It didn't compute.

Desire of the magnitude she'd encountered with Spider was totally alien to her experience. But she recognized that it was lust, plain and simple, and she refused to allow lust to win out over good sense. No, it was best that she not correct his mistaken assumption that she was married. She treasured the special friendship that had developed between them, but it was crucial that she and Spider remain friends and nothing more. When Vicki returned and helped her get this nightmare straightened out, she would be going back to Virginia to resume her life there.

With his head leaned back against the wall, Spider sat in a hard plastic chair molded for a much smaller person. Stretching out his legs, he crossed his feet at the ankle, tucked his fingers under his armpits, and stared at the tip of his boots.

While he waited at the Department of Public Safety for Anne to finish her driver's test, he had plenty of time to think. And, as usual, his thoughts focused on Anne. There was nothing to do but admit it: He was crazy about her. Without making any effort, she had twisted his heart around her finger.

The door opened, and Anne came out wearing a big smile as she walked toward him.

"I did it," she squealed, waving a new license in her hand.

He couldn't help but grin as he unfolded from the plastic chair and stood. "I'm proud of you, sugar. I think this calls for a celebration. How about a beer and a hamburger at Fuddruckers?"

She giggled. "Is your stomach all you ever think about?"

He looked her up and down, and one corner of his mouth curled into a suggestive message. "No."

She gave him a playful swat. "I thought we'd settled that issue."

He laughed and hooked her arm through his. "Just kidding, sugar. Just kidding."

Anne was still riding high as she gamely tackled a giant cheeseburger with all the trimmings. "Can you believe that I made a perfect score on my driver's test? I was a little nervous when I had to fudge on the application—I guess you could tell from the way my hand was shaking—but I did it!"

Spider chuckled and took a swig of beer. "I'm proud of you, darlin'. I never doubted for a minute that you could handle it. Now eat up. I've gotta get back to the shop to meet a production crew from the ad company. We're going to shoot some TV commercials at the Parlor this afternoon."

"How interesting! I've never seen a commercial filmed. May I watch?"

He ducked his head and drew wet circles with his beer bottle. "Nah, you'd probably be bored. Molly's planning to take you shopping this afternoon."

"Why, Spider," she said, giving a wry grin, "I believe you're trying to get rid of me. What sort of commercials are you going to do?"

"Just some stuff tied in with the holidays in February," he mumbled. "Are you about ready to go?"

Burgers finished, they drove back to the Parlor. Anne was smiling and animated on the trip home. Just looking at her gave him a warm feeling. If she was happy, he was happy.

At breakfast when she'd talked about finding another place to live, he'd felt as if he'd been poleaxed. He didn't want her to leave. In fact, he thought, he'd like nothing better than to have her around permanently. But the complications.

Of course, the big numero uno always looming in his mind was that she was married. Although eventually that could be worked out. He didn't imagine she would stay hitched to that slimeball she was running from forever. In the meantime, he would keep his promise to her and his hands to himself. It might cause a little pain, but pain he could handle.

It didn't take a genius to figure out that there were a passel of other problems, too. Anne had *big* trouble. But until this friend of hers got back in town or until she learned to trust him, there wasn't a damned thing he could do to help her out of whatever mess she was in. All he could do was be patient, stand by her, and be her friend. He could take the pressure off and keep her safe behind him.

Molly Painter, the short, perky young woman who worked part-time for Spider, was anxiously awaiting their return.

Spider peeled two hundred-dollar bills from his money clip and handed them to Anne. "Will that be enough, squirt?" he asked Molly.

Molly rolled her blue eyes. "Give me a *break*." He handed her three more and Molly nodded.

"Here," he said, giving her another. "See if you can find some cowboy boots and a western shirt."

"What in the world for?" Anne asked.

"The rodeo's coming up, sugar. Everybody dresses up for the rodeo. And buy something fancy." He peeled off another bill and grinned. "A present from me."

Anne started to argue, but he seemed so pleased with himself that she smiled and thanked him. Spider was the most generous man she'd ever met—not only with material things, but also with his time and concern. No wonder he had so many friends.

She stuffed the money in her purse, mentally adding the cash to the figure she owed Spider. At the moment, seven hundred dollars seemed like a fortune, but only a month ago she would have paid that much or more on a single sports outfit without giving it a second thought.

After she and Molly made a quick check of Anne's meager wardrobe to determine what clothes would be needed, they said their good-byes. As they buckled their seatbelts in Molly's little red car, Anne said, "I don't see how I can afford to buy too much."

Molly laughed as she zipped out of the parking lot. "You don't know the places that I do. I'll bet you've never been to an outlet store or a resale shop."

"No, but Spider and I did go shopping."

"Oh, that's fine for jeans and stuff, but the

stores I have in mind sell a different kind of merchandise—the kind you're used to."

Anne tensed. "How do you know what I'm used to?"

Molly shrugged. "I'm in clothing, remember? I recognized the quality of your silk blouse and wool slacks. Designer labels. Trust me, for what you paid for one blouse, I could have bought half a dozen similar ones for the same price."

"*Half a dozen*? Really?"

"Yep. It takes more time to shop, and you have to know where the bargains are." She grinned and gave her short, dark hair an exaggerated pat. "Lucky for you, I'm an expert, dahling."

Anne laughed at the saucy comment. "I appreciate your help, Molly."

"No problem. I'll use you as a class project. An entire wardrobe for seven hundred dollars."

Anne doubted that it could be done, but she did need only a few things, enough until Vicki returned. After all, she had closets full of clothes in Virginia.

Molly made a quick exit off the freeway, then twisted through a maze of streets before she pulled up to a large warehouse building. "Let's try this place first. They usually stock on Monday mornings, and they have the best selection in town."

Racks and racks of clothes filled the gigantic room. Anne's mouth must have dropped open, for Molly giggled as she headed down an aisle with Anne in tow. They stopped at a long row of suits.

"I figured we ought to start with something basic. What size are you?" Molly looked her up and down. "About an eight?"

Anne nodded and Molly began flipping through suits like someone possessed, pulling out one, then another, holding them up to Anne, shaking her head, then putting them back.

"Bingo!" She jerked a camel-colored suit from the rack and held it against Anne. "Perfect!"

Anne fingered the well-cut fabric. "It feels like cashmere."

"It is. And only seventy-five bucks."

"Seventy-five dollars?" Her eyes widened in surprise. She'd noted the distinctive label. "It can't be. Is something wrong with it?"

Molly grinned and stuck her nose in the air. "Last year's collection, dahling. Think you can live with it?"

Anne giggled and lifted her nose in the same pose. "I suppose I can make the sacrifice."

Catching the bargain fever, Anne raced around with Molly, gathering up things to try on. When they stopped, arms laden with possibilities, they sought out a dressing room. Only a frazzled, olive-green curtain separated the large community dressing room from the showroom.

Lined with mirrored walls and racks for hanging, the area was teeming with women in various states of undress. Shy about disrobing in such a public place, Anne whispered, "Isn't there someplace else I can use?"

Molly shook her head. "Sorry. It's the price we pay to keep overhead low. If she can," she whispered, inclining her head toward a woman trying to squeeze her size eighteen hips into a size twelve dress, "you can."

For an hour Anne tried clothes on and took them off, with Molly passing judgment, keeping tabs on her calculator, and occasionally running out to rummage through a bin of five-dollar scarves and belts.

At last they settled on several outfits. "These are wonderful," Anne said as she tied her shoelaces. "And I can't believe the prices. But are you sure we haven't spent more than seven hundred dollars?"

When Molly had punched in the last number from the price tags on her calculator, a broad grin spread over her gamine face. "Nope. Would you believe that all this is only three hundred and seventeen dollars?"

Anne's mouth dropped open. "You're kidding!"

Scooping up a load of clothes, Molly wiggled an eyebrow and said, "Stick with me, babe. You ain't seen nothing yet."

Laughing, Anne said, "I can't imagine anything more."

When their purchases were stowed in the car, Molly said, "Next stop, Bankruptcy Shoe Warehouse. Charge!"

Molly's excitement was contagious, and Anne couldn't remember when she had enjoyed shopping more. She'd been to countless showings and sipped wine in the finest houses in Paris, Rome, and New York, but she'd never had more fun than she was having looking for bargains in Houston.

They bought shoes and boots for unbelievable prices, and at a resale shop they found the fancy dress Spider had instructed her to buy. While they were there, Molly rummaged through the used items and got excited when she pulled out a red jumpsuit in soft challis.

"Oh, I don't think so," Anne said. "I've never worn red well." But Molly insisted she try it on. The supple fabric felt wonderful, but she frowned at the seductive image in the mirror. All she could think of were red satin sheets, and her face flushed and her palms went damp. "It's just not me."

"Oh, but it is. It's funky. And it's sexy. Spider will go into orbit. My special guy would."

"Molly, there's nothing like that between us. Spider and I are just good friends."

"Uh-huh," Molly said, as if she didn't believe a word Anne said. "I've seen the way he looks at you. To die for! I've worked at the Pawn Parlor for over a year, and I've never seen Spider so goosey over a woman. You're a lucky lady. Spider's great."

In spite of Anne's arguments, she ended up buying the jumpsuit. Thirty dollars *was* a bargain, she rationalized. And the quality was excellent.

They wandered through a wholesale jewelry store, and Molly filled their basket with a mound of costume jewelry, most of which Anne felt was much too gaudy, but her perky companion insisted the pieces were the "in" thing and perfect for her new look. "Funky" was her favorite word. And even though Anne wasn't used to jangling and clunking and flashing as she walked, she had to admit that the things were kind of fun. Maybe being blond made the difference.

A pair of earrings caught Anne's attention, and she stopped to look at the small gold spiders with tiny blue jewels for eyes. "Oh, look. These would be perfect for Spider."

"Why don't you get them? He'd love it."

"Do you think so? I thought maybe there was some significance to the cutlass. I've never seen him wear anything else."

Molly shook her head. "Not that I know of. He used to wear a gold hoop sometimes, but I think he lost it."

On their way out the door, Molly said, "Well, we did it." She checked her watch. "And in four hours and sixteen minutes. It must be a record." Her face lit up with a smile. "We have sixty-three dollars left. What do you want to splurge on? Another purse? Sexy lingerie? I think we ought to go back for the red polka-dot shoes we saw at the warehouse. They would be fabulous with the jumpsuit."

"I'm pooped. Why don't we save it for another time?"

Winter's early darkness was falling as they cut across a poorly lit area to the car, parked a distance away. Anne felt the hairs on the back of her neck prickle, and she looked over her shoulder, searching the shadows. Being out at night made her feel nervous and vulnerable.

With the sun gone, the air was chilly and she shivered. A gust of wind rattled a discarded sack and sent it sliding across her feet. She kicked it away and shivered again.

A car roared to life, and she jumped. How silly, she chided herself, to startle with every little sound. But still, she'd be glad to get back to the safety of the Parlor. And Spider.

Suddenly, an explosion pierced the quiet. Anne

screamed. Her shopping bag went flying as she grabbed Molly and dragged her down, flinging them both flat against the ground.

Molly yelped and tried to get up, but Anne held her fast.

"Stay down," Anne hissed.

"What's going on?"

Terrifying images flooded her memory. "He's found me again! He's trying to kill me!"

"Who's trying to kill you?"

"Preston. Or his hoodlums." Another loud bang exploded. "Oh, Lord!" Hysteria clung to the edges of her sanity, scrambling to rise up and take over her reason. "They must have been following us all day, waiting for their chance. We've got to get out of here. We've got to run!"

"Anne, listen to me. That was a car backfiring, not a gun."

"A car?"

"Yes."

"Are you sure?"

"Positive."

Anne went limp and the breath rushed from her lungs. "Oh, Lord, I feel like such a fool."

Molly helped her up. "You're shaking like a leaf. Is somebody really trying to kill you?"

Anne nodded.

"Are you okay now?"

Her knees were wobbly, but she brushed her jeans and managed a semblance of a smile. "I'm fine. I'm sorry I acted like an idiot. You must have thought I'd lost my mind."

Molly laughed as she picked up the shopping

bag. "It occurred to me there for a minute." They walked to the car in silence. When they were safely inside, she turned to Anne. "I suppose it's none of my business, but I've always been the nosy type. Why is somebody trying to kill you?"

"It's a complicated story, and the less you know, the better. I don't want to endanger my friends."

"Can't you go to the police?"

Anne shook her head. "I told you it's complicated. Things will be straightened out in about three weeks. Until then, I'm taking refuge with Spider."

Molly looked puzzled, but Anne appreciated her not pressing for answers. "Spider will take good care of you. He won't let anything happen."

"I know. And, Molly, please don't say anything about this."

The young woman pulled an imaginary zipper across her lips and winked. "Not a word." She started the car, then looked over at Anne. "We still have the sixty-three dollars. Are you sure you don't want to get the polka-dot shoes? They'd be really funky."

Anne laughed, warmed by Molly's obvious attempt to restore the mood of their trip. She, too, wanted to forget the incident. "I'm very sure. The only thing I can think of that I'd like to have would be some perfume, but I can do without it."

"What kind do you like?"

"I usually wear Bal a Versailles, but sixty-three dollars would barely buy a whiff."

"But it would buy some toilet water, and I know the perfect place to get a good deal. It's on the way."

Anne didn't want to make another stop, but she didn't protest. She only wanted to go home. Home. Was she beginning to think of a storeroom in a pawnshop as home? Or was it Spider's being there that made her feel secure?

In a few minutes, Molly wheeled the little red car into a beauty-supply store that advertised special prices on all the best-known fragrances.

While Anne selected a bottle of toilet water, Molly sprayed a tester of Bal a Versailles on her wrists, sniffed, looked at the display wistfully, then sighed and turned to Anne. "Anything else you need from here?"

"I don't think so." She sprayed her wrists as well and sniffed. "You like this scent?"

"I love it. It's so . . . romantic. Maybe if I hint to my boyfriend, he'll buy some for my birthday."

"Is it coming up soon?"

"In May. While we're here, I need some shampoo." Molly went to another aisle.

Anne did a quick computation in her head. Even at bargain prices, she didn't have enough money to buy two bottles, but she wanted to give her new friend something special for helping her. She selected a small purse-size spray, deciding it would do her until Vicki returned. The larger bottle she would wrap and give to Molly.

By the time they reached the Pawn Parlor, the backfiring-car incident had been relegated to the far corner of her mind. They were laughing and talking, with Molly keeping her amused with anecdotes about working in a pawnshop.

"I can't remember when I've had such fun. Thanks, Molly."

"I've had fun, too. And I won't say anything about, you know, the other stuff. Say, it looks like the ad people are still here. Maybe we can watch them film." She motioned to a large van parked in front of the shop with Fast Track Productions scrolled across its side.

Boots was standing outside the door when they walked up, arms laden with packages. "They're shooting the last one now," the lanky redhead told them. "If you're real quiet, you can watch."

He held the door open, and they tiptoed inside, trying not to let the sacks rattle.

"Step into my parlor, sweet thing," Turk's mellow voice called.

"Keep that bird quiet! We're about to shoot."

The place was crowded with crew and equipment and lights on tripods focused on an area in the rear of the shop. Anne eased around a drum set and craned her neck to see over the shoulder of a burly man in a baseball cap who stood in her way.

Her eyes widened, her jaw dropped, and every package in her arms crashed to the floor.

Six

"Quiet back there!" a frizzy-haired man in a purple jersey yelled.

Anne froze and stood as still as a mouse, her attention riveted to the center of attraction. Her initial shock was gradually giving way to horror as she watched Spider run through his lines. Surely, he didn't intend to appear in a television commercial like that!

Mortification flooded over her, and she glanced over to Molly, whose pursed lips were twitching. "What is he supposed to be?" Anne whispered to Molly.

"Cupid," she managed to squeak out, then clamped her hand over her mouth to strangle her laughter.

Anne's head swiveled back around, and her gaze swept over Spider, from the silver cutlass swinging to his bare feet. The only things in between were a gold quiver of arrows slung across his back and a pair of brief running shorts, red satin, like his sheets. The quiver's gold strap bisected a thick patch of dark hair that curled over his broad, bare chest and trailed down below his navel quite a distance before its path was obscured by his scanty covering.

A makeup girl ran up and blotted a few spots here and there, then ran back off.

"Okay, let's have quiet. Roll tape," the frizzy-haired man commanded. "Action!"

Spider leaned toward the video camera. A cocky grin lifted one side of his stubbled face. "Friend, are you a little strapped for cash to buy your sweetie a valentine?"

A laugh built in Anne's chest and tried to fight its way past her throat. She clamped her teeth together, but it burst forth in a muffled snort. Another louder one followed. Then a whole series erupted.

"Cut, cut!" The director glared at her. "Lady, you've ruined the whole take!"

Anne felt a flush creep up her neck and heat her cheeks.

Spider peered out from the lights. His face thunderous. The director paled, and the room went dead still. "That lady," Spider ground out, "is a special friend of mine, and if she wants to laugh, she can. Do you understand me?"

The man nodded, and said, "Let's take a break everyone."

Spider sauntered over to where Anne stood, mouth agape, heart pounding. She, like everyone else in the room, believed Spider was murderously angry.

But for her, he smiled, and his eyes took on a special softness. He reached out and brushed the back of two fingers along the curve of her cheek. "Sorry about that, sugar. The guy has no manners. Did you and the squirt have a good time? Did you buy lots of pretty clothes?"

For the longest time, Anne could only stare up at the muscled mountain standing in front of her. Then she managed a tiny nod.

"I'm sorry I laughed."

"Shoot, you're supposed to laugh. Being funny is what makes folks remember the commercial." Grinning broadly, he stood there in his outrageous outfit without even a glimmer of self-consciousness. "I make a hell of a cupid, don't I? You should have seen me earlier in the powdered wig and satin britches."

She tried to imagine the sight, and a smile twitched at her lips. "A powdered wig?"

"And a tricorn hat and a little hatchet." He placed one hand over his heart and said, "I cannot tell a lie. Spider Webb has the best deals in town."

Her smile blossomed into a chuckle. "I don't know where you find the nerve."

"I get a kick out of it. Hell, I write most of my own stuff, don't I, Roscoe?" he asked, turning to the man in the baseball cap.

Roscoe grinned. "That he does, ma'am. They're so bad that they call them high camp, and he's won a couple of awards for my agency. His crazy spots have made him a bigger celebrity than playing football ever did. I think it's because his legs are so pretty."

Roscoe glanced down at Spider's legs, thick as tree trunks and covered with hair, and hooted with laughter. Spider gave him a playful cuff.

"Anne, this wise guy that I'm making rich and famous is Roscoe Osborne, owner of the ad agency and old running buddy. Roscoe and I go way back. Anne Webb, distant cousin and special lady."

She offered her hand and Roscoe took it. "Pleased to meet you, ma'am. I'm sorry that the director mouthed off at you that way. We won't be using him again."

Before she could protest, Spider said, "He does good work, and everybody's entitled to one mistake. I don't think he'll make the same slip again."

Roscoe laughed. "I don't think he will either. You scared the sh—" he glanced at Anne and sobered "—stuffing out of him."

Spider insisted that Fred bring a chair so that she could sit near the action while they taped the last spot. Anne looked around for Molly, but she had left her armload of packages with Boots and slipped away sometime during the course of things.

"Won't it make you nervous for me to watch?"

"Nah. I'm a born ham. You can be my muse." He readjusted the quiver. "Let's roll it, Percy."

"That's Perry, Mr. Webb," the director corrected meekly.

Anne stifled a snicker.

Spider took his place under the hot lights. Even in his ridiculous garb, he was mesmerizing. The outfit only accentuated his blatant virility. A drop of sweat rolled down his neck, disappeared in the black curls of his chest, then reappeared as it slowly slid along the corded plane of his abdomen. Spellbound, she watched the drop descend to-toward the low-slung shorts covering—she flushed and went warm all over as she remembered what they covered.

The makeup girl ran out, brushed Spider's hair, blotted and powdered, then ran off the set. The drop was gone.

"Roll tape! Action!"

Spider took the cigar from his mouth and gave Anne, who was sitting by the camera, a devilish grin. "Friend, are you a little strapped for cash to buy your sweetie a valentine?"

Her mind wandered to red satin sheets, and before she knew it, Perry was yelling that it was a wrap. The lights were struck and the cameraman started putting away his equipment.

Anne blinked up at Spider. "Is it over already?"

"Yeah, they're only thirty-second spots. We did three of them today. We'd have been finished sooner, but I had something I needed to do before we got started. I want to show you something, but let me get out of this outfit first."

"I'll put my packages away while you dress."

"No, you stay right here. Don't move till I get back. I've got a surprise for you."

When Spider left, Roscoe wandered over to talk to her. "What did you think of our spot?" he asked.

"It was . . . interesting."

He grinned. "Yeah, I know what you mean. But he comes across great on TV. The camera loves him. And his crazy commercials have made him a sort of cult figure around town. I keep telling him that with his background, he ought to go to Hollywood and be a movie star. He'd be a natural."

"His background?"

"Yeah, you know he got a degree in communications. With honors. And when he was with the Raiders, he made a lot of commercials on the West Coast, for everything from tires to underwear. He was good. I always figured that when his playing days were over he'd get into sports broadcasting or pictures, but . . ." Roscoe shrugged.

This new information about Spider had surprised her. And, upon reflection, she was disappointed in herself. She'd always been impatient with people who jumped to conclusions before they had adequate information, and now she was guilty of the same offense. It seemed that there was a great deal more depth to Spider Webb than she'd assumed. And it occurred to her that she really didn't know very much about him at all.

They chatted until Spider, dressed in his usual jeans and T-shirt, strode into the room. His eyes were bright and energy crackled the air around him. "Are you trying to make time with my lady, Roscoe? I may have to tell Trish on you." Grinning, he gave Roscoe a poke in the belly.

"Aw, she'd never believe it. We still going to get together this weekend?"

Spider threw his arm around Anne's shoulder and pulled her against him in a playful hammerlock. "It depends on my friend here." He looked down at her. "You wanna drink some beer and boogie?" He swiveled his hips and bumped twice against hers.

Catching his mood, she laughed. "Fine with me."

"Well, I'd better be shoving off," Roscoe said. "Nice to meet you, Anne." He tipped his baseball cap. "Spider, the valentine spot will be ready to start running Wednesday, and the Washington's Birthday and rodeo ads are scheduled for next week."

"See you Saturday night, Hoss," Spider called to Roscoe as he left. To Anne, who was still penned in his arms, he said, "You look tired." He brushed at her bangs as his eyes scanned her face. "Did you and the squirt buy the stores out?"

"The stores still have a few items left, very ugly and not in my size," she teased, smiling up at him. "Molly is a demon shopper. I can't believe that we bought so much for the money. As a matter of fact, I have twelve dollars left over. Want to help me carry packages?" She looked around the shop, quiet now except for two customers with Fred. "Where are my things?"

"Boots stashed them in your room. Come on," he said, taking her hand and pulling her after him. "I want to show you my surprise."

"What is it?"

"Now, if I told you, it wouldn't be a surprise, would it?"

"You seem to be in especially good spirits," she said as he led her from the shop and down the short hall toward her storage room-bedroom. "Have you been drinking?"

He laughed. "Nah, sugar. I'm always wired after I shoot commercials. Must be the thespian in my soul."

She shot him a you've-got-to-be-kidding look, and he laughed again. At the door of her room, he paused and, with a sweep of his hand, allowed her to precede him.

Two steps in, she stopped in her tracks, awestruck at the transformation. Gone were the sewing machine, the saddle, and the stacks of other goods that had been shoved around the perimeter of the room.

The water bed was still there, but instead of the jungle pattern and fake fur, the mattress was covered with an old-fashioned print, flowers and butterflies, in dusky rose on white with touches of blue, green, and wine. Ruffles along a matching quilted coverlet brushed the floor around the bed, the head of which was piled high with variously shaped pillows. Two walls were covered with the same print fabric, as was a round table next to the wine velvet Victorian settee she recognized from the shop.

Against one wall was the Venetian armoire from Spider's room; against another was a Victorian writing table and a round, ornately carved piano stool. There were two Tiffany Favrile glass and bronze lamps, one beside the settee, another on the writing table. Shaped like clusters of lilies, they cast a soft glow over the delicate furnishings and the plush scatter rugs on the floor.

Walking to the writing table, Anne ran her finger over the intricate inlay and rosewood surface. She picked up the top of the jade censer from Spider's office, which now rested on one side of the table.

It was filled with peppermints.

Her throat constricted and she blinked her eyes several times. She looked into the gilt-framed mirror above the table to see Spider's blue eyes watching for her reaction.

"Is it okay? Do you like it? Lisa said the pretty little desk we found out back would do for a dressing table—for your makeup and stuff—and she said anything would be better than that god-awful zoo on the bed. She didn't have time to do everything, but we decided that you'd want to put the finishing touches on. I told her—"

Anne turned, touched her fingers to his mouth, and smiled. "I love it. It's beautiful. And the nicest surprise I've ever had."

His face split into a king-size grin. "Lisa said she thought you'd like it. I called her while you were taking your driver's test this morning. She's a professional decorator."

"Oh, Spider, you shouldn't have hired a decorator."

"You don't like it."

"I *do* like it, but the expense . . ."

He shrugged and grinned. "A couple of bottles of beer. Lisa and her husband, Wally, are—"

"—friends of mine," they finished together.

"You'll meet them this weekend," he told her. "Wally and I played football together my last season on the Oilers. He retired last year. They're nice folks. Now let me see what's in these sacks." He gathered several of the packages Boots had left by the door and dumped them on the bed.

"Are you really interested?" She began pulling

garments from the bags while he picked up the rest of the load.

"Sure I'm interested. What did you get?"

Spider leaned against the armoire, stuck his fingers under his arms, and watched while she took out all her purchases and laid the clothing on the bed. He nodded and made appropriate comments for each item.

He was so dear, pretending to be interested in her clothes, that Anne wanted to hug him. And how many men would have even considered the decor of her bedroom as something worthy of their time? For all his macho posturing, Spider Webb was a teddy bear.

Striding over to the bed, he picked up the jumpsuit and held it up against Anne. His mouth curved into a slow smile. "I think this is my favorite."

Anne laughed. "Molly said you'd like it."

"The squirt's right. It's sex-ee." He wiggled his eyebrows. "What else?" He looked at the unopened bags.

"Just some shoes and some costume jewelry."

He grimaced and snapped his fingers. "A jewelry box. I forgot. I think I know where there's one. I'll be right back."

She hung her clothes in the armoire, put away the new shoes, and set the two boxes of perfume on the writing table. When she opened the bag of jewelry, she saw the gold spider earrings and pulled them out. Her gift seemed so insignificant compared to all he had done. She was still debating whether to give them to him, when he came back into the room, dusting a large tortoiseshell box with the tail of his T-shirt.

"I don't know what this is, but it's kind of pretty. Will it do?" He set it on the desk, and she opened it.

"It's a tea caddy, and quite a lovely one. It will do nicely. Thank you, Spider. You've done so much, I don't know how to thank you."

He reached out to cup the side of her neck with his palm. "Don't worry about it, sugar." His voice was low and husky. "I just want you to feel safe and be happy here."

The warmth of his touch, the titillating nearness of him, sparked a yearning, deep and gnawing. More than anything, she wanted to take a step forward and snuggle against his solid body, have him wrap his arms around her and hold her close. She clenched her hands into fists and something bit into the flesh.

Looking down at the forgotten earrings she held, Anne said, "I got something for you today. It's not much, but I saw them and thought of you."

"You bought something for me?" His tone was incredulous.

She nodded and gave the box with the earrings to him. "After all you've done, I'm embarrassed that it's so little." He took them and looked down at them for a long time, his face expressionless. "They're little spiders. They're only gold-filled, and I know you usually wear the cutlass, but . . ."

He looked up, his eyes glittering like blue diamonds. "They're beautiful, Annie. And the nicest gift I've ever received."

A slow smile spread over his stubbled face, and he moved toward her. His head dipped just a fraction, then paused. A medley of emotions played over his face as his gaze met hers.

Taking the cutlass from his ear, he handed her the box. "Put the new one in for me, sugar." He sat down on the piano stool and pulled her between his outspread knees.

Heat pulsated from his body, warmed his scent, and bombarded her with sensation. His hands, resting lightly on her hips, seemed to burn through the fabric of her jeans. Her fingers trembled as she put the gold spider in his earlobe. Her mouth dried; her breath quickened. Sensual awareness, potent and ready to ignite, hung between them like a curtain of smoldering gauze. Pictures clicked and flashed through her mind. Red satin sheets. Nude, passion-slicked bodies. Blue eyes and a hungry mouth and skin on skin.

She tried to pull away, but her feet wouldn't function.

He looked up at her, his pupils wide and black, his gaze blatant with desire, but he didn't move. It seemed like forever that they stayed there, unmoving. Finally, he sucked in a deep breath.

"Thank you, dear friend." He stood, gave her a quick peck, and stepped back. "You hungry? I'm starved. I think I could eat about ten pounds of pork ribs, slow-smoked over hickory and dripping in barbecue sauce. How about you? You like Texas-style barbecued ribs?"

She smiled at his valiant effort. She knew he wanted to kiss her. More than kiss her. Didn't she want the same thing? "I don't know if I've ever eaten any."

"Well, you haven't lived until you've tasted Shorty's barbecued ribs. Powder your nose, and we'll go wrap our eyeteeth around some."

Spider's mouth watered as he caught the distinctive smells of hickory-cooked meat drifting over the parking lot. After that business with Anne and the earrings, all his appetites were revved up. He was one big walking, talking ache. He'd rather be filling her than his belly, but maybe indulging one hunger would take the edge off the other.

He laughed at himself as he steered her toward Shorty's. Who was he kidding? A plate of ribs was a poor substitute. Just having her beside him turned his gut wrong-side-out. He was almost to the point of not caring if she was married. Almost.

The thick, smoky aroma hit them full in the face as they walked through the door of the crowded barbecue joint. A small place with not more than fifteen scarred tables crammed together, it had rough wooden floors and neon beer signs on the walls. Willie Nelson's twanging wail and the click of pool balls in the side room mixed with the drone of a full house.

"Hey, Spider!" several people called.

"Hey there, partner," he called back, giving each a wave and a smile.

"Do you know all those people?" Anne asked as he seated her at an empty table in the corner.

"Only a couple of them to speak to."

She smiled. "You really are a celebrity."

"Nah, I'm just a good ol' boy that a few folks recognize. Hey, Shorty," he said to the five-by-five man who approached. "How's the ticker?"

"I've lost fifty pounds and had to give up cigars, but it's still ticking." He grinned and swiped one beefy hand on his big white apron, adding another sauce smear across his girth. "How's it going, man?" He held out his hand.

Spider took the hand that was offered. "Can't complain, Shorty." He introduced Anne to the jovial man, and Shorty tipped his wool plaid golf cap to her.

"What can I get you folks tonight?"

"Two big rib plates and a pitcher of beer."

"Comin' right up."

When the hefty man strolled away, Anne asked, "Does he have heart problems?"

Spider nodded. "He had a bypass a few months ago."

"I'm not surprised. Everything in here must be loaded with cholesterol. I've noticed that you eat too much of it, too. You need to eat more fish and green vegetables."

He grinned, tickled that she was fussing over him. "I guess I need a wife or a mother around to crack the whip over me. You interested in the job?"

"I'm too young to be your mother," she said, suddenly becoming very interested in the salt shaker.

He let it pass.

"Roscoe said you have a degree in communications."

"I do. Does that surprise you?"

She was quiet for a minute. "A bit, I suppose.

He said you could have had a career in sports broadcasting or in the movies."

"Would you like me better if I was Don Meredith?"

"Who is Don Meredith?"

He laughed. "Another Texas boy. An ex-Cowboy who went the TV-and-movie route. Sugar, I know all the ten-dollar words if I want to use them, and I clean up pretty good, but New York and LA don't have a thing I want. This ol' boy was glad to get back to Houston. And after I learned what I was doing, I found that I liked the pawnshop business. I don't have to wear a monkey suit if I don't want to, and I don't have to suck up to anybody. Maybe I could make more money doing something else, but I've got enough for the things I need. And I like knowing that my friends are real people who accept me for what I am, not a bunch of parasites who latch on to me because I've got a big bankroll or my name in lights."

Anne nodded and stared off into space. "Wealth isn't what it's cracked up to be."

"You've got that right, sugar." He paused as Shorty's oldest son served their food. "All I need is a big plate of ribs, a pretty lady to share it with, and I'm happy."

She reached across the table and laid her hand over his. "You're a good man, Spider. And the best friend I've ever had."

He beamed. "Thank you for the compliment. You're special to me, too." He patted the soft, slender hand, then touched the earring in his lobe. The memory of how it got there started him swelling all over again. Before she could see the agony of desire in his face, he forced a carefree grin. "Now eat up, darlin'. When you taste this stuff, you're going to think you died and went to heaven."

Her big brown eyes widened as she looked down at her platter. "I can't eat all this!"

"Give it your best shot. I'll handle the leftovers." He tucked the corner of a big napkin in the neck of her sweater and did the same with his own. "There's no way to be neat about this. Just dive in."

He picked up the biggest rib and proceeded to gnaw the meat off the bone, trying not to laugh when she gingerly lifted one sauce-laden piece and, holding it daintily with two fingers, nibbled at the smoked pork.

"You know, this *is* good."

"Told you."

Even though he polished off three to her one, she soon got the idea and attacked the barbecue with the same gusto as he did. He wanted to laugh and kiss her right in the middle of Shorty's Barbecue Joint.

He nearly went crazy watching her eat. Every time she licked her lips, he wanted to groan and say, "Do that to me, babe." She got a little spot of sauce on her chin, and he watched it for the longest time. If he'd done what he ached to do, he'd have climbed over the table and removed it with a long, slow swipe of his tongue.

With less than half her meat gone and barely a dent put in the potato salad and beans, Anne sat back in her chair and sighed. She held her sauce-covered fingers up and said, "I can't eat another bite." She looked down at her bib. "And there's not a clean place left on my napkin. Yours is still white. How'd you do that?"

"Like this." He leaned over, captured one of her hands, and brought it to his mouth. With careful strokes of his tongue, he bathed her index finger, then, looking into her eyes, drew it slowly into his mouth and sucked.

She swallowed a little gasp, but she didn't pull away. When he started to move to the next finger, she suddenly jerked her hand from his.

"I've got the idea." Pushing back her chair, she said, "Excuse me, I'm going to the ladies' room."

He watched the sway of her cute little bottom as she beat a hasty retreat. Every swing of her hips fanned the flames higher. His fingers fondled the bit of gold in his earlobe. Two hours on his Nautilus machine tonight wasn't going to help a damned bit.

Seven

It was Saturday morning. Anne sat at the yellow table in Spider's kitchen waiting for her nails to dry. Molly, who had been thrilled with the toilet water Anne had wrapped and given her, had taken pity on Anne's poor polishing technique and taken over the task.

Preparing for a function at the White House would have produced less anxiety. It was silly to be so jittery, she told herself. She had met and liked Roscoe and his fiancée, Trish, who had done her hair. Lisa, the decorator, and her husband, Wally, who had played football with Spider, were joining the group. She was sure they were all nice people. But even though the activity that Spider had planned with his friends was still hours away, she was as nervous as she had been for her first prom date.

"What does one wear to drink beer and boogie?" she'd asked Spider the day before.

He'd laughed. "We're not going anywhere fancy. Wear something comfortable. How about that red jumpsuit? The sexy one?"

Molly had agreed that it was perfect for the occasion, yet she still felt somewhat out of her element and unsure of herself. But at least she felt safe. She'd been here for over a week and there was nothing to indicate that Preston had traced her to Houston. If her car or identification had been found, Preston's trackers would have been poking around by now.

Yes, she was safe from her stepbrother for the time being, but Spider was another story. Though overtly he had been the soul of propriety, she could feel the sexual attraction between them smoldering only a millimeter beneath the surface. She knew that if she pushed the tiniest bit, he would have her between his red satin sheets in a blink. The trouble was, she was having a hard time not dragging him there. Every day, she found Spider's heady sensuality harder to resist. Every night, her dreams were blatantly erotic and filled with images of a black-haired rogue whispering in her ear and doing incredible things to her body. Red satin sheets would be her downfall. She was obsessed with them.

Glancing over to the drier, she watched the red culprits tumble round and round in the drum. The sheets and her emotions had a great deal in common.

The day seemed to drag by. Spider was working

with his accountant, and the shop was busy. As she walked through the displays checking for hidden treasures, she noticed the little gray-haired lady in the mink cape.

"Hello," Anne said to her. "Mrs. Bremmer, isn't it?"

The woman smiled. "Yes, and you're Anne."

"May I help you find something?"

"Oh, no, dear, I'm just browsing. Don't mind me." The grandmotherly woman smiled sweetly, and Anne returned her smile.

Since there was so much activity in the Pawn Parlor, Anne decided to poke around the warehouse attached to the back of the shop. Something caught her eye as she wandered through the stacks and shelves of merchandise. She laid down her clipboard and dragged a step stool to a corner shelf. Standing on tiptoe, she pushed aside a radio and reached for the porcelain clock that had been half-hidden.

"What are you *doing*?" Spider shouted.

Startled, she teetered, but big hands clamped around her waist and held her steady. "You almost scared me to death. I wanted to look at that piece up there." She pointed to the ornate clock and stand. "I think it may be a Meissen."

He lifted her down to the floor. "I'll get the clock." He retrieved the dusty piece and set it on a crate. "Why didn't you call Boots or me? You shouldn't be climbing around this mess."

"Spider, I'm perfectly capable of lifting a clock. All week you've been treating me as if I'm helpless and fragile. I'm not. I'm supposed to be working for you, but how am I going to earn my keep if you do everything for me?"

"Sugar, you've more than earned your keep this week. Why, your commission on the green candy dish alone will more than repay the money I loaned you."

"It's not a green candy dish; it's an Oriental jade censer. And what commission?"

"Ten percent of the profit on anything out of hock that's sold."

Eyeing him suspiciously, she asked, "Is this a policy you invented for me, or does it apply to everyone?"

"Why, sugar, you can't honestly believe I'd invent something like that just for you."

He looked innocent. Too innocent. She wanted to say yes, she certainly did believe he would. Since she'd been here, he had become more and more solicitous of her. In fact, his behavior bordered on hovering. But she sighed and decided to ignore the issue for the moment.

"In any case, the jade isn't sold yet. The gallery's client is coming in Monday to see the censer and the rug."

"Oh, yeah, I forgot the rug. See, that's another commission. You can afford to take it easy. Why don't you go paint your nails or something."

"Spider, I've already polished my nails, and I'm not sure that it's a Chichi prayer rug that I found."

"Sure it is. It looks just like the picture in the book you got from the library. You're more than earning your keep, darlin'. I'd never thought of calling the galleries and offering them a commission on sales." He took her by the arm. "Why don't we go get an ice-cream cone? I'll bet you like pistachio."

With the same slick style he'd used all week, he tried to coax her away from the work she'd been trying to do. None of her arguments seemed to make a dent in his determination to treat her like an honored guest instead of an employee. This time she put her foot down.

"Spider, I don't want any ice cream. I want to clean this clock and check its markings. It reminds me a great deal of one my mother had on the mantel in her bedroom. If it is a Meissen, and in good repair, it's very valuable."

He frowned at the porcelain piece, lavishly decorated with flowers and cherubs and surmounted by a Roman god. "I can't imagine why anybody would pay good money for this thing. It looks like something you'd win at a carnival. I think it's been here since we took over the place, but if you want to clean it up, I'll help. Where do you want it?"

He picked it up in one hand, and Anne squealed at his cavalier treatment of what might be a rare prize. "I'll take it," she said, retrieving the clock and holding it carefully. "Spread that towel on the worktable, please."

When the towel was spread, she placed the piece on the table and began removing years of dust and grime. While she worked, Spider, fingers tucked under his armpits, leaned against a refrigerator and watched.

"You said your mother had a clock like this?"

"Mmmm."

"She have a lot of this kind of stuff?"

"Quite a bit."

"What's a thing like that worth?"

"I'm not sure, but if it is a Meissen, I'd estimate somewhere between three and five thousand dollars."

"Good Lord!"

She laughed. "They aren't carnival prizes."

"You told me your mother died last summer. Did she leave everything to you?"

"Yes, she did." Hands stilled, eyes narrowed, she looked up. "What is it you're asking? If I have a house full of valuable antiques, why am I penniless and hiding out in a Houston pawnshop?" With a pang she thought of her own gallery, which she'd created on her own.

He gave her one of his slow, sexy grins, but there was a you-caught-me twist to it. "Now, sugar, don't get testy. I know you don't like to talk about your business, but I have a natural curiosity. You ought to know by now that you can trust me."

Looking down at the clock, she resumed her cleaning. Yes, she trusted him. She wasn't ready to tell him everything, but she did owe him at least part of the story.

"I am the sole heir to my mother's estate, including the house and furnishings. But I don't have access to them. Unfortunately, Preston lives there, and he controls everything I have."

"Oh, yeah. *Preston*." He spat the name in disgust. "I don't see why you don't get a good lawyer and kick the slimeball out."

"That's easy for you to say, but—" She stopped and forced herself to take a deep breath. "When Vicki gets back, that's exactly what I intend to do."

"Sugar, you don't have to wait for Vicki. Hell, this town is crawling with hotshot lawyers. Why, I've got a friend—"

"*I'll* handle this, Spider. In my own way. The subject is closed. Hand me that book on porcelains."

He grinned. "Yes, ma'am."

Spider knocked on the bathroom door. "You about ready, Anne?"

She gave her blond hair, freshly washed and brushed into the style she'd grown to love, a final pat, took a deep breath, and opened the door.

His eyes raked over her once, then went back for seconds. He let out a low wolf whistle.

"Are you sure this looks okay?"

She chewed her lip and fiddled with the long purple-and-red paisley scarf that belted the jumpsuit. Never in her life had she been so worried about her clothing, but then, she'd always worn classic styles of understated cut and neutral color. Why she was so nervous, she couldn't imagine, since Spider was dressed in his usual boots and jeans with a black T-shirt and his faithful leather jacket.

"Turn around."

She made a slow pivot. She could almost feel his gaze burn through the supple red challis.

"Darlin', if you looked any better, they'd have to

cart me away in a body bag." He gave her a slow smile that almost blistered her nail polish.

She laughed and hooked her arm through his. "Spider, you do wonders for a lady's ego."

"Got your dancin' shoes on?"

She held out her foot to show him her taupe wedges. "But I've never done any—what's it called?"

"Kicker dancing. I guess they don't have many honky-tonks in your neck of the woods. Don't worry, you'll catch on."

She picked up her purse and wrap from Spider's bed, managing to accomplish the feat without a lingering glance at the red sheets. Doing a shuffling sashay, he linked his arm with hers, and they left the room with Spider bouncing and singing a nasal, "Deep within my heart . . ."

A few minutes later, they climbed out of the Silverado and walked through the crowded parking lot to a pink stucco hacienda with a tile roof and Christmas lights in the bushes. A bright yellow sign over the entrance proclaimed it to be the San Antone Rose.

Thumping country music and shouts of "Ahh-hh-ha!" hit them as the door opened. The energy of the room bounced off the walls and set adrenaline surging through her blood.

Three bars, liberally decorated with neon cacti and maps of Texas, were doing a brisk business. People were everywhere, and a disc jockey spun records from behind a stuccoed wall covered with Tex-Mex graffiti. Most of the place was so smoky and shadowed that for a moment Anne couldn't see clearly. Spider bent near her ear and shouted, "Hang on to me, and we'll find the others."

"Hey, Spider!" someone yelled from across the room.

They peered through the crowd to see Roscoe waving his baseball cap, and, with a bit of judicious twisting and weaving, they found their way to the table near the dance floor. Anne greeted Roscoe and Trish, then smiled as Spider made introductions to Wally and Lisa.

Barely were they seated when a cocktail waitress in a cowboy hat stood ready to take their orders. "It's Saturday night. Longnecks are fifty cents for another hour."

"Beer okay?" Spider asked Anne over the bustle of bodies, loud conversation, and floor-shaking music.

"Fine," she answered after checking the drinks of the others, all of whom were holding tall bottles. With antlered deer heads, longhorns, and Mexican posters mounted on the walls, the atmosphere hardly seemed appropriate for the white wine she preferred.

It was difficult to talk over the noise of the room, but she thanked Lisa, a redhead in a kelly-green sweater and slacks, for the decorating help. "I really appreciate it."

Lisa gave her a broad smile. "I was glad to do it. I hope you like it. God knows, the shape that room was in, anything would have been an improvement. Sorry I didn't have more time, but Spider said it was a rush job. I'll come one day next week and help you finish it if you'd like."

"I'd love it."

"Come on, sugar, let's do a little two-stepping." Spider grabbed Anne by the hand and pulled her up.

"But I don't know how."

"Nothing to it. Watch my feet," he said as they headed around the railing of the dance floor. He did a few steps and said, "You do that and I'll do the rest. It's easy once you get the rhythm."

After a couple of false starts and lots of laughter, she discovered it was easy. And fun. They were soon two-stepping around the room with the counterclockwise flow of the other dancers. Spider's lead was strong and sure, and he was an excellent dancer.

"You're really good," she said.

"Sure I'm good. I had years of practice tippy-toeing away from all those beefers in the pads and helmets."

"Modest, too."

He laughed, twirled her around, then brought her back to his arms.

Between sipping beer and laughing with the others at their table, Spider taught her to polka, and Roscoe insisted on showing her the Texas swing. Wally, who was even taller than Spider and must have weighed three hundred pounds, led her into a waltz. He was amazingly graceful. In no time at all, she learned to recognize songs by Willie and Waylon and Reba and Randy.

"It's time for a pit stop," Trish said, and the three women left for the ladies' room, the third trip in as many hours. "It's the beer," Trish explained to Anne, dodging a shoe-shine girl in skin-tight jeans and cowboy hat who was doing a show of her own.

"You and Spider make such a cute couple," Lisa said as they washed their hands. "And the way he acts, he must be crazy about you. I've never seen him quite so taken with any of the other—"

Trish poked Lisa and rolled her eyes.

A strange emotion, quick and clutching, seized Anne. If she hadn't known better, she'd have thought she was jealous. Silly, of course, since she and Spider were only friends. Anne managed to laugh at Lisa's faux pas and they returned to the table.

Everyone danced, tried their hand at several of the games in the corners of the room, and drank more beer. Anne couldn't remember when she'd had so much fun. Spider's friends were genuine, caring people who gathered her into their intimate circle as if she'd always belonged.

When a slow ballad began, Spider grabbed her hand. "Come on, they're playing our song."

Anne laughed as she trailed behind him to the dance floor. "You idiot, we don't have a song."

He pulled her into his arms. "We do now."

"I think I've had too much beer," she said, snuggling into the perfect spot against his body. "I'm getting very relaxed."

"That's okay, sugar. I'll take care of you. Just lean on me."

Even as big as he was, she seemed to mold exactly into the contours of his frame. His head bent slightly and her forehead resting on his cheek, they moved in slow, synchronized rhythm. So close that not a speck of daylight showed between them, she followed his lead as if they'd been dancing together all their lives.

Spider took the soft hand he was holding, brought it to the nape of his neck, and left it there. Both arms around her, he pulled her tight. He closed his eyes and savored the exquisite torture of Anne in his arms. God, she felt good. He would pay for this later, but for now, he was in hog heaven. If the song went on forever, it would suit him fine.

"You smell like flowers and sweet, sweet woman."

Sighing, she rooted her forehead against his cheek and wiggled her body against his, trying to get closer. He almost went up in smoke.

"Spider?"

"Hmmmm?"

"I think I'm getting turned on."

"I know I am."

"Is that good?"

"Probably not."

"Do you mind?"

"Hell, no."

She sighed. "Me neither."

They stayed on the floor for another song. Couples two-stepped around them, but they swayed on to the beat of their own slow, seductive music. By the time the song ended, beads of perspiration rolled from his hair and he was rock hard and ready. If it had been anybody but Anne, he would have dragged her out to the parking lot and made wild love on the front seat of the Silverado.

But it wasn't just anybody. This was Anne. *Married!* a part of his brain shouted. *Remember your promise.*

Promises, hell, he was on fire! And hurting bad. He'd never in his life wanted anybody the way he wanted her. Every curve of her body was burned into his memory. The smell of her made his mouth go dry. And she wanted him; he knew she did.

But he forced himself to smile and say, "It's late. You about ready to go home, darlin'?"

She stared up at him with big brown eyes gone dark and sultry. "I'm ready when you are."

She sat snuggled against Spider as he drove home. He'd barely said a word, but she knew he wanted her. She'd have to have been a fool not to have felt the evidence that had pressed against her when they'd danced. And Anne Foxworth Jennings—oops! Jennifer Anne Webb—was no fool.

Despite all her best intentions to keep their relationship platonic, she had changed her mind. Maybe there wasn't a future for them, but there was certainly a mind-blowing present. And she meant to take advantage of it. A man like Spider might only come along once in a lifetime, and she didn't want to pass up the opportunity.

She laid her hand on his thigh.

He flinched.

She giggled.

"I like your friends, Spider. They're lots of fun."

"They like you, too. They're good people."

She slid her hand up farther. He grabbed it and

pushed it back down. "Woman, what are you doing to me?"

She giggled again.

"I think you had too much to drink."

"Uh-uh." She cozied against his shoulder, rubbing her cheek across the leather of his jacket. No wonder he liked to wear the jacket; it was sensuously soft. And if she lived to be a hundred and three, she'd never forget the delicious, virile smell of him.

He stopped the truck. "We're home."

Handling her more delicately than if she were fine porcelain, he helped her out of the pickup. As she watched him unlock the front door and turn off the alarm, she studied the dark set of his jaw, the sinuous curve of his lips, the deftness of his big hands and long fingers. She could imagine those hands on her bare skin, and desire for him uncoiled low in her body. This was the night that she would make love with the sexiest man on earth. And damn the consequences.

"Step into my parlor, sweet thing," Turk said.

Anne laughed. "I'll never forget the time I first heard that. I was terrified."

"And now?"

She smiled. "I'm not terrified."

He locked the door behind them and reset the alarm. Anne wondered if they would go to his bedroom or hers. Should she shower and put on the slinky gown she'd bought at the resale shop? Perhaps they would simply undress one another slowly, kissing, touching, exploring as they went.

With a hand at her back, he guided her through

the shop and down the hall. Her heart pounded, and her breath was shallow. She'd didn't think she could wait for a shower. She wanted him now. They stopped at her door, and she looked up at him. He smiled.

"Good night, sugar." He gave her a brotherly peck on the cheek. "Sleep tight." He turned and started back down the hall.

Stunned, she called after him. "Where are you going?"

"I'm going to work out on the Nautilus equipment for a couple of hours."

Humiliation still stung as Anne stepped out of the shower, dried, and pulled on her sexy new gown. She muttered to herself as she stomped through Spider's room and across the hall to her own. She climbed into the undulating water bed and yanked the covers over her head. But she couldn't sleep.

She heard Spider when he came down the hall; she heard the shower running; she heard the muffled oaths as he punched his pillow.

She was wide-awake. And she had to go to the bathroom. It was the beer. She tried to ignore the urge, but it grew more desperate.

The only way to the bathroom was through Spider's room. She got up and tiptoed to the door. Everything was still, so she eased across the hall, trying to be as quiet as possible.

When she'd finished her business and was sneaking out of his room, Spider growled, "I'm awake."

"Sorry," she said. "It's the beer."

For a long time after she left, Spider lay there inhaling her lingering fragrance. He ached for her so badly that he was tempted to handcuff himself to the bed to keep from getting up and going after her.

An hour later, he was wide-eyed. He was obsessed with the idea of running his tongue over every square inch of her skin. Lord, he couldn't take this much longer. He was going out of his mind!

He heard her tiptoeing to the bathroom again. Involuntarily, his gaze fixed on the closed door. When it opened and he saw her, he felt like he'd been clipped by King Kong. She was wearing something long and flimsy, but she might as well have been naked. The light behind her made the gown transparent, and he could see every lush dip and curve.

"Damnit, woman!" he roared. "What are you trying to do to me?"

"I'm sorry. I was trying to be quiet. It's the beer."

He slung his arm across his eyes and muttered a string of curses. "I'm dying. You're killing me."

The bed dipped and he looked up to see Anne sitting there, a worried look on her face. Light from the bathroom outlined her like a halo. She was a blond-haired angel; she was a honey-mouthed temptress. She was *his*, and he wanted her. Now.

She put her hand on his bare chest. "Spider, what's wrong?"

"What's wrong? I want you so bad it's tearing my guts out. That's what's wrong."

She chuckled. "Is that all?" Her hand made a lazy circle. "That's easily remedied."

He grabbed her wrist. "But I promised."

"I release you from your promise."

She bent and touched the tip of her tongue to his nipple. It streaked over him like a flash fire, and he almost bowed double.

Holding her face in his hands and his control by a hair, he said, "Darlin', you're married. I don't mess with married women, remember? Never have. I had it done to me, and I damned sure don't mean to do it to anybody else."

She smiled. "Sugar," she drawled, "I'm not married."

"You're divorced?"

She shook her head slowly. "I've never been married."

"Then who in the hell is Preston?"

Eight

"Your *stepbrother*?"

She nodded and raked her fingers through the silky black curls on his chest.

His eyes, heavy-lidded and sparking blue fire, bored into hers, and his voice was a deep growl. "Sugar, you've got a hell of a lot of explaining to do." He grabbed her under the arms, and she laughed as he dragged her across his body and flung her onto the cool red sheets beside him. With a lightning-fast move, he rolled and trapped her, one hand propped on each side of her head. "Later."

Lips parted and tongue poised, a feral noise rumbled deep in his throat, and his mouth covered hers in a searing, devouring kiss. She moaned and her arms clamped around his broad back. The hot kiss went on and on amid groans and insatiable tongues thrusting and touching and plunging.

He tore his lips from hers and kissed and licked a frantic path down her throat. His tongue was like fiery velvet. And when it reached the rise of her breasts, the sensation arched her back and wrenched a breathy moan from deep inside her.

Nuzzling the soft swell, he dragged the straps of her gown down and pushed the filmy fabric to her waist. His tongue drew a hot, wet trail along the underside of each breast, circled and circled each hardening peak.

"Oh, darlin', you taste like sweet heaven."

He drew one nipple into his mouth and gently suckled. Each pull tugged at her sanity and heated her blood. She gasped from the wonder of it, and her palm pressed and slid down his back to his tight, bare buttocks, then back up again.

"Let's take this off," he said. "I want to look at you." She lifted her hips; he peeled off the gown and tossed it to a fluttering heap on the floor.

His eyes and his hands swept over the length of her. "I've dreamed of this. I've lain awake in this bed and imagined you here. Lord, you're even better than my dreams."

She tried to speak, but she was breathless with longing for him. His every movement was erotic. He was taut muscle and raw, dark beauty. And magnificently aroused. All she could do was whisper his name.

His eyes flashing and his lips parted, he knelt at her feet, ran his hands up the outside of her legs, and watched his dark fingers move over her pale skin. Grasping her ankles, he lifted her feet to his mouth. He kissed the ball of each foot and set her heels, one on each of his shoulders.

His fingers began a slow slide along the insides of her legs. Ankles, calves, knees, thighs, higher; then he lingered, his thumbs gently brushing the length of exposed flesh and soft curls. Strangely, she felt no shame or embarrassment, only intense hunger and a heady sense of feminine power and pride.

She whimpered with the delicious agony of his touch as he worshiped her body with his hands and eyes.

Shuddering, he closed his eyes and sucked in a trembling breath. "Babe, I wanted this to last. I wanted to touch and taste every bit of you, but you're wet and ready, and I can't wait much longer."

He opened his eyes and looked at her with pupils gone wide with desire. His magnificent body glistened with the fine sheen of arousal.

"I want you, too, love," she whispered. "Now."

Rolling to the edge of the bed, he reached under the mattress. In a moment he was back, nudging apart her legs, bending to kiss her lips with a savage yearning.

"Woman, you set me on fire," he groaned as he scooped her buttocks in his big hands and lifted her from the slippery satin sheets.

He tried to enter her slowly, but Anne wrapped her arms and legs around him. "Fill me," she urged. "Please."

With a hard thrust, they were joined. Flesh in

flesh, and caught in a wildfire. Plunging and meeting, demanding and taking, there was nothing
quiet or gentle in their lovemaking. It was raw
and savage and earthy. He drove hard and she
demanded more, rising to meet and move and
twist and cling, seeking greater pleasure.

She bit his shoulder and scraped his back. Wet
with passion and slick with striving, she urged
him on to a release that seemed just beyond her
grasp.

He slipped a hand between them to stroke an
aching spot. Her whole body lit, glowed, then burst
into an explosion of exquisite sensation. She
sucked in a cry and arched to the source of her
pleasure.

"Sweet love," he murmured, pausing until the
spasms of bliss subsided into soft ripples. Then
he began to stroke again, with his hand, with his
body.

"Oh, Spider," she gasped in surprise as the
pleasure began to mount. "It's happening again."

He chuckled and licked his tongue across her
mouth before he plunged it between her lips. When
her climax burst once more, he cried out with
her, his face a mask of exquisite agony, his body
bowed, tense and still, as if focused on the pleasure ripped from his nerve endings.

They lay quiet, still joined. His forearms held
some of his weight off her, but he didn't move for
the longest time. His head was nestled in the
crook of her shoulder, and his ragged breath tickled the base of her throat. She stroked his back,

loving the feel of its broad expanse beneath her fingers.

She teased his left earlobe, smiling at the gold spider she felt there. He'd worn nothing else since she'd given it to him. She ran her fingers through his thick hair and pushed a few errant strands from his forehead. Still he didn't move.

"Spider?" she whispered, sliding her hands along the breadth of his shoulders.

"Sugar, I don't think I can go again right now. Give me a couple of minutes."

She giggled and swatted his backside. "Get off me, you hulk. You're heavy."

Putting his arms around her, he rolled away, taking her with him so that she lay atop him. He fingered strands of her hair and touched her lips. "I'm sorry I was so rough with you, darlin'. I wanted you so damned bad, it got out of hand. Did I hurt you?"

She shook her head and chuckled. "I was as rough as you were. I don't know what got into me."

He wiggled one black eyebrow and grinned. "I do, darlin'. Me."

Laughing, she gave him a playful swat. "Bad pun."

He wrapped both arms around her and held her close. His voice was thick with emotion as he said, "Lord, Annie, I'm crazy about you." After a moment he added in a lighter tone, "And you're hell on wheels in bed."

"That's not a very romantic thing to say." She

poked him in the ribs and he flinched. "You're ticklish!"

"No, I'm not."

But he was. She delighted in torturing him as they tussled in the tangled satin sheets until he was laughing and begging for mercy.

They showered and laughed and made love. They straightened the bed and slept with Spider holding her close to him, as if he never wanted her to move from his side. Sometime after dawn they awakened and reached for one another again.

During that time, Preston wasn't mentioned. But when Anne awakened later, she found Spider lying beside her, his head propped by his elbow, his blue eyes watching her.

"You have some explaining to do," he said. "Want some coffee first?"

She nodded.

"I'll fix it."

While he was gone, she slipped on her gown and went to the bathroom. Brushing her tangled hair, she tried to decide what to tell him and how much to tell him.

The truth. All of it. He deserved no less.

Feeling chilly in her thin gown, she draped his black leather jacket around her shoulders, then straightened Spider's bed and sat down on its edge to wait.

She suspected that he was going to be angry that she had lied to him about being married, and the idea of his being angry or disappointed in her hurt. Absently, she stroked the worn leather of the jacket. It occurred to her that his reaction was extremely important. She was very close to falling in love with Spider Webb, pawnbroker and ex-football player, a man far removed from the life she'd always known. It was a sobering, scary thought. When had she come to care so much for this man? Was it after last night? Or had it gradually sneaked up on her without her even being aware of it?

Maybe he'd understand when she explained the whole story.

Dressed only in black jeans, zipped but unbuttoned, he came back carrying a tray. His hair was tousled and already dark whiskers shadowed his jaw, but one piercing look from his diamond-blue eyes and her heart turned over.

"Why are you out of bed? I brought coffee. And some toast I fixed while the coffee dripped."

"It looks like you used a whole loaf of bread."

He grinned. "I'm hungry. And I've got to keep my strength up." Setting the tray down, he stacked pillows against the headboard and held back the covers for her. "Get in. It'll keep your tootsies warm."

When she did, he tucked the fur cover around her, put the tray across her lap, and spread a towel under her chin. Dragging the step stool up close, he slathered butter and grape jelly on a piece of toast and insisted on feeding her every bite of it.

"What about you?" she asked.

"I cheated. I had a couple of pieces in the kitchen."

"No, I mean, aren't you cold?"

A slow, cocky smile lifted one side of his mouth. "I told you I was hot-natured."

She laughed, and he poked another bite of toast into her mouth.

When their coffee cups were empty and only a few crumbs dotted the toast plate, he set the tray on the floor. Resting his bare heels on a rung of the stool, he propped his elbows on his knees, clasped his hands together, and leaned forward.

"Now, we talk."

Anne looked at him for a moment, then took a deep breath. "Are you angry with me?"

"Do I look angry?"

"No, but I . . . lied to you."

"Yes, you did, sugar. And I want to know why."

"Well, at first, I had to explain why I was using a name different from the one on my driver's license. It seemed like a logical explanation."

He nodded. "And later?"

"Spider, this is later. I trust you now. I . . . I care about you. So I told you the truth. I didn't have to."

"What about this Preston character, your stepbrother? Is he really after you?"

Anne nodded and told him about her mother's death, Preston's proposal, and the conversation she had overheard between Preston and Bradley, the deputy director of the FBI, the night she came home. Spider's jaw tightened until the muscles twitched and his eyes went as cold as a Canadian winter.

"Son of a bitch! He ought to have his eyeballs roasted over a slow fire."

"I would provide the matches," Anne declared. "I was so scared after I heard what he said to Bradley that I hid in the hall closet until Preston went upstairs. I knew that I had to get away somewhere, calm down, and think what to do. Somehow I kept my wits about me enough to open the safe and stuff every file I could find into a briefcase. I figured that the deputy director's 'extremely sensitive' one that Preston alluded to would be among them and might give me some leverage. Then I grabbed my purse from the hall table, sneaked out to the garage, and took off in my car. I went to an all-night diner a few miles away."

"You should have called the police."

"I did. The chief. Fool that I was, I told him everything."

"Didn't the bastard believe you?"

"Oh, he believed me. He told me to calm down and stay put, he'd be there in a few minutes. I was sitting in a back booth, drinking a cup of coffee and trying to stop shaking, when I saw him get out of a car in front of the diner. Preston was with him. I ran out the back way. I'd parked my car in the shadows on the side, and they didn't see me leave."

"Why in the hell did the idiot call Preston?"

"They play golf together. And I hadn't looked at any of the files then, but Bradley's was not the only sensitive one in the safe. I discovered later there were a score of them, and Preston had a particularly nasty dossier on the chief's daughter. I was almost hysterical by then, and it was after midnight, so I drove to Georgetown to my friend

Meg's house. I know I wasn't making much sense, but Meg and her husband Howard put me in their guest room. I couldn't sleep, so I went downstairs to get a glass of milk and overheard Howard talking on the phone. I gathered from what he said that Preston had called my friends and told them that I was having a breakdown."

"And they believed him?"

She gave a bitter laugh. "Preston is very powerful and very persuasive. The story gets worse." She shivered.

Spider climbed into bed with her, drew the covers around her chin, and held her close. "Sugar, you don't have to talk about it right now if it upsets you."

"No, I want to tell you all of it. Needless to say, I sneaked away from Meg's house. I just drove until I was exhausted. I ended up in Norfolk. I checked into a hotel and slept for about twelve hours. Room service provided my meals, and a boutique downstairs brought clothes to me. For three days, I didn't go out of the hotel. That's when I read the files in the briefcase."

"The briefcase in there?" He inclined his head toward the organ against the wall.

She nodded.

"I knew they should be put in a secure place, so I decided to take them to the bank and rent a safety-deposit box. It was too late to do it that evening, so I was going to do it the first thing the next morning. Then it occurred to me that I needed to make copies. I looked through the yellow pages and found a copy shop that would be open late, so

I went out. I was about to get in my car when somebody shot at me. If, just at that moment, I hadn't dropped my keys and bent to pick them up, I'd be dead. I jumped in the car and drove away. A second shot shattered the rear glass."

"Oh, darlin'." Spider laid his cheek on the top of her head and hugged her to him. "I won't let them find you. You're safe here with me."

"Oh, Lord I hope so, but I can't stay here forever. And Preston or his men always seem to find me." She threaded her fingers through the hair on his chest, taking comfort from his strength and the steady beat of his heart.

"After I left Norfolk, I drove to someplace in North Carolina and spent the night. While my car window was being replaced, I remembered a friend who lived in Raleigh and called her. Marmi insisted that I come to her house. She sounded a bit strange, but I decided I was being paranoid and drove to Raleigh that afternoon.

"Thankfully, I had the good sense to be cautious. I left my car in a lot and took a taxi. The driver must have thought I was crazy, but I insisted he circle the block twice. The second time around I noticed a car parked down the street with two men in it. One of them I recognized as a man who worked for Preston. I knew then I couldn't trust anybody. Preston must have called everyone in my address book."

"Surely, darlin', you had friends who wouldn't have been taken in by that slimeball."

"I've never been a gregarious person, Spider. I've never had as many friends as you. Acquaintances, yes, but, with my mother's illness and my work, social time was limited. But I did think I had a few good friends, until I found myself in desperate need of one. I considered Meg a friend. Yet she believed Preston over me."

He tipped her chin and looked into her eyes. "I'm your friend, sugar. You can count on me for now and always." He smiled. "Believe it."

"I do."

Hugging her close again, he said, "Tell me the rest of it."

She settled against his chest and stared off into space as she remembered her frantic flight. "Thinking I could lose myself in the city, I spent the night in a small town in South Carolina and drove to Atlanta the next day. I checked into a hotel, bought clothes, and tried to figure out what to do. Finally, I decided I'd be safer in Europe, so I booked a flight, stored my car, and went to the airport. Somebody shot at me again as I was getting out of the taxi."

"My God, darlin', you must have been terrified!"

"I was, but I think the taxi driver was even more frightened. I ducked back inside, and he took off with the door still open."

"How did they find you?"

"I didn't figure that out until I had picked up my car and was halfway to Birmingham. Credit cards. Naive fool that I was, I'd left a trail a child could follow. Hotels, restaurants, dress shops, gas stations, the airline—everywhere, I charged things. Even for phone calls, I used my credit card. And for someone with Preston's resources, access to computer records is simple." She slapped her forehead with the heel of her hand. "Stupid, stupid, stupid."

Spider stilled her hand and brought it up to kiss its palm. "Darlin', you weren't stupid. You were an honest person who'd never had a reason to think about devious tricks or hiding out. At least you caught on before they found you."

She nodded. "I had some traveler's checks and a little cash, but I knew it wouldn't last long. Then I remembered Vicki. I hadn't seen her for years before we ran into each other in France last fall, but I knew immediately that she was the perfect person to help me. I started for Houston. Keeping off the major highways and spending nights in small towns, I zigzagged my way here. But Vicki wasn't home, my money had run out, and you know the rest."

"Sugar, you've been very brave." He kissed the top of her head, stroked her arm, and said, "I don't think we should wait for Vicki. I think we should call the authorities right now. I have a friend in the DA's office who—"

"No!" she cried, pulling away and looking at him with pleading eyes. "You don't understand. I can't trust anybody! You can't believe the people Preston controls."

"Babe, I know he's scared hell out of you, but it can't be that bad." A smiling hint of patronization shaded his tone. "Surely—"

"Damn it, Spider Webb, listen to me! You haven't seen what's in that briefcase! Even if I could trust the police, I dare not let the files be seen by just anyone."

"Sugar—"

"Damn it, I said, don't you condescend to me!"

She scrambled out of the bed and stalked to the organ. Using both hands, she tugged at the scarred instrument, trying to move it away from the wall.

Spider bounded from the bed. "Here, sugar, let me do that."

She glared at him and lifted her nose. "*I'll* do it, thank you very much."

Putting her whole body into it, she yanked and tugged and pulled until the organ rolled away from the wall. She knelt in front of the safe and put her hand on the dial. But she was so angry that she couldn't remember the combination. At that moment she'd have sooner eaten worms than have asked for Spider's help. She took a deep breath and tried to calm herself. The numbers wouldn't come.

"You need some help?"

"I can't remember the combination."

"You want me to do it?"

She ground her teeth together. "Just wipe that smug look off your face and give me the numbers."

When the safe was open, she clutched the briefcase to her bosom and marched back to the bed, with Spider dogging her trail. He held back the covers and she climbed in. He climbed in beside her. She scooted over so that they didn't touch. He put his arm around her and dragged her back.

Keeping her spine very straight, she opened the briefcase and pulled out several of the files. She thrust them at him and said, "Read. Many of the names you'll recognize. Those you don't, I'll identify. The one on top is a key member of the Cabinet."

His eyes widened. "As in Washington?"

She nodded.

For several minutes, only the rustle of pages and an occasional profane expletive from Spider broke the silence of the room.

"Who is this?" He held up a page.

She leaned over and read the name. "Federal judge."

"And this?"

"Wife of a senator from the Midwest. And the next one is a member of the Federal Reserve Board. All of the people in the files, or a close family member, hold positions of great power and influence."

Spider let out a whistle and leaned back against the brass headboard. "I don't need to read any more. I already feel like a Peeping Tom. This is heavy stuff. Some of these folks could go to prison."

Anne nodded. "Or be publicly disgraced. Preston was very thorough. He must have been collecting information for years and using my family's money to do it. He's been blackmailing some very important people. Oh, I suspect he exacted his tribute in political favors and information instead of money, but I have no doubt he was using this information for blackmail. Imagine the scandal for our government if all this came out at once. There could be tremendous repercussions."

"Sugar, somebody needs to know about this. And Preston belongs in jail."

"I know that, but I can't just walk up to the White House and knock on the door. I dare not go to the FBI. And at least one of Preston's victims is highly placed in the Justice Department."

"What are you going to do?"

"I'm going to wait for Vicki. She's a very bright attorney, honest to a fault, and her father is an ex-senator who is a close friend of the President. They'll know how to handle this."

Spider stuffed the files back in the briefcase. "No wonder you were so scared, sugar. You were in a hell of a spot."

"It frightens me just to think about all of it again."

"I'll put these back in the safe. And then," he said with a wicked grin, "I'll see what I can do to take your mind off it."

For the next several days Spider did everything he could to keep her mind off Preston and danger. He succeeded.

Sometimes with friends, sometimes alone, they went to movies, the zoo, a basketball game, and he even took her to a museum or two and swore that he wasn't bored. At night they made love and slept close together in his big brass bed. But he barely let her out of his sight. It was difficult even to go to the bathroom without Spider tagging along. She couldn't as much as start to open a jar of pickles without him grabbing it out of her hand and doing it for her.

While she appreciated his concern for her safety, and while she was growing fonder of him each day, his solicitude did sometimes rankle a bit. When she tried to talk to him about it, he'd drawl, "Ah, sugar, I like to spoil you," and kissed her until she forgot her arguments.

About midmorning of the end of her second week in Houston, both of them were in the shop. The Parlor was busy. It seemed that everybody in town had seen his Cupid commercial and had come in. Spider was writing a pawn ticket for a customer who was hocking his shotgun, and Anne was showing the Erté bronze to a potential buyer, a referral from one of the galleries.

"I think this is just the thing for my wife's birthday, little lady. How much?"

When she told him the price, he whipped out his checkbook. In less than five minutes, she'd made a sale. When the man left carrying the statuette, Anne waved the check at Spider. He grinned and winked.

She was feeling really good about herself. With the sales commission from the jade censer, the prayer rug, and the Meissen clock, she had paid Spider every penny she owed him and gotten her watch out of hock. He hadn't wanted to be repaid, but she'd insisted. She even had money in her new bank account. Not bad for someone who had only twenty-eight cents when she'd arrived in Houston.

The next thing she wanted to do was find her

own transportation. Of course, Spider took her anywhere she wanted to go, but it wasn't the same as having her own car. She couldn't afford to buy one, but she could rent one for the week or so before Vicki came home.

Turk announced another customer, and she looked up to see the delivery boy from the florist next door. He was carrying a huge arrangement of pink roses and baby's breath.

"Flowers for you, ma'am." He set the vase on the display case, tipped his cap, and grinned.

"For me?"

"Yes, ma'am. I hope you enjoy them," he said and left.

She reached for the card. *Happy Valentine's Day to my sweetie*, it said. *Love, Spider*. She thought of him in his cupid costume and laughed out loud.

"It looks like you have an admirer," a voice said.

Anne glanced up from the card and recognized the gray-haired lady in her mink stole. She smiled. "Hello, Mrs. Bremmer. May I help you with something?"

"Oh no, dear, I'm just browsing." She leaned over to smell the roses. "Lovely, just lovely. You and Spider make such a nice couple."

The little woman patted Anne's hand and wandered away. Anne looked for Spider, but he wasn't in sight. Smiling, she picked up the vase, breathed in the sweet fragrance of the roses, and carried the arrangement to her room. Pink roses were her favorites.

Placing them on the writing table, she stepped

back to admire the bouquet. Strong arms wrapped around her middle and drew her back against a body she'd come to know intimately. Spider leaned over her shoulder to nibble her ear.

"You like the posy?"

"Mmmmm," she said as he nibbled lower. "Very much. Thank you."

"How about you put on your fancy dress tonight, and we'll go somewhere classy for dinner."

"I'd love to." She tilted her head as his mouth did wonderful things to the side of her neck.

"Can you think of any way we can kill time until then?"

She laughed. "Why is it that I suspect you already have something in mind?"

"Psychic?"

"Hardly. But I'm going to have to take a rain check. Lisa is picking me up for lunch, and we're going shopping."

"You going to get me a valentine?"

"Oh," she said, feigning nonchalance, "I may. And while we're out, I'm going to check into renting a car."

"Why do you need a car?" He sounded offended. "I'll take you anywhere you need to go."

"I know you will, and that's very sweet of you, but I'd like to have one of my own. You have a business to run; you don't need to act as my chauffeur every time I want to go to the library or a gallery."

"But I like taking you places."

Twisting out of his grasp, she turned to face him. "Spider, I want a car of my own. I don't like depending on someone to do everything for me. It makes me feel like a leech. I'm perfectly capable of driving myself."

"You can borrow my pickup any time you want, sugar." He grinned.

She didn't grin back; she rolled her eyes in her best imitation of Molly and said, "Give me a break."

"Then I'll buy you a car. What color do you want? Blue? I've got a friend who'll give me a good deal on a Mercedes. Would you like a Mercedes? Or maybe you'd rather have a BMW. They're cute little cars."

She put her hands on her hips and glared at him. "Spider, you are *not* going to buy me a car. I am going to rent one. The subject is closed."

Nine

"Just a minute!" Anne called, twisting to look over her shoulder at the back of her dress and wishing for a full-length mirror. She wanted to look especially nice tonight.

Had it been a conscious or unconscious decision that had made her select the blue silk jacquard at the resale shop? Blue was Spider's favorite color, and she had to admit that the dress and the color were flattering. She straightened the matching cummerbund and put on her pearls.

Spider had even provided a mink stroller for the occasion. "It's mine now," he'd told her. "The sixty days were up day before yesterday. You'll need something warm tonight. It's going to be cold."

"But it was almost eighty degrees today."

"Texas weather is always crazy. There's another norther moving in. Besides," he'd added with a grin, "the coat matches your hair."

She draped the jacket over her arm, picked up a card and a small package with a blue ribbon from the desk, and opened the door. Spider was waiting for her.

To say that she was stunned was an extreme understatement.

He was Adonis in a charcoal-gray suit. His white shirt emphasized his dark good looks, and his silk foulard and handkerchief were a silvery blue that matched his eyes. His clothes were urbane, well tailored, and worn with casual ease.

Her gaze traveled from polished black shoes to tamed black hair, still curved below his collar in back but lending, with the spider earring, a tempting touch of savagery to his elegance.

She gave a low whistle and smiled.

He grinned. "I was about to say the same for you, gorgeous." He gave her a peck on the nose. "You look beautiful. But then you always look beautiful. Ready to go?"

Holding the package and the card out, she said, "I wanted to give you this first. Happy Valentine's Day."

"For me?" He looked as pleased as a child on Christmas morning.

He opened the card and smiled as he read every word of the sentimental verse. He untied the ribbon on the small package and laughed at the key chain with the gold cupid hanging from its ring. Hugging her, he said, "Thank you, sugar. This is perfect. It's the best valentine I've ever had."

"I'll never think of Valentine's Day without remembering you in your cupid costume. I looked and looked, but I couldn't find one with running shorts."

He laughed again and said, "Come on, darlin', I'm getting hungry." Giving her a lecherous wink, he added, "And the sooner we eat, the sooner we can get home. I'll change into my cupid outfit for you."

"You're a crazy man," she said, laughing.

Outside, he led her to a Mercedes, blue, and opened the door. "What is this?" she asked.

"My new car. I got a real deal on it. You like it?"

"Where is your pickup?"

"Oh, I still have it."

She narrowed her eyes. "What are you going to do with two cars?"

He shrugged. "I thought maybe you might like to drive this one."

"Spider Webb, I told you that I'm going to rent a car. I'm picking it up tomorrow."

"You can cancel it, sugar. No use in letting this one just sit idle."

Anne wanted to stamp her foot and yell at him. And she never yelled. "You are, without a doubt, the most overbearing—"

He silenced her with a quick kiss. "Darlin', you can fuss at me later. Let's go eat."

By the time they arrived at the Inn on the Park, he had coaxed her out of her pique, and she was laughing. If she had been surprised by Spider's stylish dress, she was doubly so when the maitre d' of La Reserve greeted him by name and when Spider ordered Corton-Charlemagne—eighty-two or eighty-three, he'd said offhandedly—with their dinner. The difference in him was amazing.

Looking up from the raspberries and cream they were having for dessert, she studied him for a moment. The elegantly dressed, polished man across from her could easily fit into an embassy reception or a gallery showing. His kind of natural manner and self-confidence lent itself to any setting.

"What's wrong? Did I use the wrong fork?"

She laughed. "You know very well you didn't. I was just thinking how comfortably you fit into these surroundings."

He looked around the posh restaurant. "It's okay once in a while. And the food's good here. Nearly as good as Shorty's ribs. Did you enjoy your dinner?"

"Very much."

"Would you like coffee or a liqueur?"

She shook her head.

He grinned. "Good. Let's go home. Eating those raspberries reminded me that there are a couple of other luscious things I'd rather taste tonight."

He wanted time to stand still, but even with Spider squeezing every minute of every hour, the week after Valentine's Day flew by. He knew he was being possessive of Anne, following too close, not giving her room to breathe sometimes—Lord knew, she'd stamped her cute little foot at him more than once—but he couldn't seem to help himself.

He hadn't known that there was a big hole in his life until Anne came along. In three short weeks, she had burrowed into his heart and become a part of him. Now he didn't know what he'd do without her. He loved her. He was about to burst with love for her. He wanted to tell her, but he wasn't sure how she'd take it, and he didn't want to scare her off.

Sometimes she hated to admit it, but she needed him. And he liked being needed. He'd do anything for her. He'd gladly walk barefoot through the fires of hell and take on the devil with a baseball bat to keep her safe and beside him for the rest of their lives. To hell with Preston Ames and those damned files.

One night, in the quiet aftermath of their lovemaking, they lay snuggled close together, replete, drowsy. Taking pleasure in the feel of her soft skin, Spider's hand slid slowly up and down her arm. He wished they could stay like this forever, content in each others arms. The thought that she might leave caused him to break out in a cold sweat. But when Vicki came back—

"Sugar?"

"Hmmmm?"

"With all the hotels and stuff you own, you've got a lot of money, don't you?"

"Quite a bit. Does that bother you?"

"Nah, not really."

"Why did you ask?"

"I thought it might bother you. Hell, I'm just a broken-down ex-jock who owns a pawnshop. I don't run with the same kind of crowd you're used to. I don't mingle with the elite at disease balls."

Anne raised up and looked at him. "What's a disease ball?"

"You know, those big charity dances where the bigwigs get gussied up in tuxedoes or Paris dresses with lots of beads and big bows and try to outdo each other." He gave a disdainful snort.

Eyes twinkling, she pursed her lips and cocked her head. "Why, it sounds like great fun to me. I think you'd look kind of cute in beads and big bows."

He growled and she giggled as he flipped her on her back and started nibbling her neck.

Anne, dressed in western garb, complete with boots and red bandanna, stood by the gun case waiting for Spider to finish with some paperwork. Wearing his black cowboy hat with a rattlesnake band—complete with rattles—pulled low on his forehead and his hair curved over the collar of his blue-jean jacket, he looked like a desperado. She smiled. A magnificently handsome desperado.

"My, my, don't you look like a regular cowgirl?" a sweet voice said.

"Oh, hello, Mrs. Bremmer. I didn't see you come in." She glanced down at her jeans and snap-front blue shirt. "Spider's taking me to the rodeo. May I help you with something?"

"No, dear, I'm just browsing. You young people have fun." The gray-haired lady smiled, settled her mink stole around her shoulders, and wandered away.

"Isn't she sweet?" Anne commented as Spider laid his arm around her shoulders. "She always seems to be browsing. Does she ever buy anything?"

Spider snorted. "Not a dime's worth. But she comes in at least three times a week to *browse*."

"Surely you can't begrudge a dear old lady's whims. Maybe she's simply lonely."

His mouth curled into an expression of wry amusement. "Keep your eye on the 'dear old lady.' You might be surprised."

"What do you mean?"

"Just watch her."

"Looking into the circular mirrors mounted high in each corner of the shop, Anne watched Mrs. Bremmer wander up and down the crowded aisles. The old lady picked up a pair of binoculars, looked around, then popped them in the oversized purse she carried.

"Spider!" Anne whispered. "She's *stealing* those binoculars."

He chuckled. "Keep watching."

Mrs. Bremmer added a camera to her purse and stuffed an electric can opener in the pocket of her mink stole before she wandered out the door.

Anne was incensed. "Aren't you going to stop her? Shouldn't you call the police?"

"Nah."

"But that sweet little old lady is a thief!"

He shook his head. "Kleptomaniac."

"But that's even worse. She needs to see a psychiatrist. You're not helping her by allowing her to get away with stealing."

Spider laughed and hugged her. "Aw, sugar, don't get your tail feathers up. She does see a shrink. Has been for a couple of years. Once a week, regular as clockwork."

"It doesn't seem to be helping."

"Sure it is. She brings everything back the next time she comes in. She thinks I don't see her."

Narrowing her eyes, she looked at him suspiciously. "How did you know about the psychiatrist?"

"The first week Pinky and I had this place, I caught her pinching a spinning reel and an answering machine. I checked up on her and found out that her husband had died the year before and she'd moved into one of the ritzy high rises a few blocks from here. Her son is the president of a bank. The second time we saw her cop something, I talked to her son, and he got her some help. I understand she's been stealing for years, but her husband always covered up for her."

"Spider, how dear of you to get help for Mrs. Bremmer. Most people wouldn't get involved. You always amaze me, though I don't know why I continue to be surprised. You're a genuinely nice person."

He struggled with a grin. "Aw, shucks, ma'am."

She laughed at his effort to sidestep the compliment. "Well, you are. Is it time to go see the pigs and cows now?"

"And the bull riders, and the calf ropers."

"And George Strait."

He sighed theatrically and picked up her suede

coat. "And George Strait. What is it with you women? What's George got that I haven't got, bigger and better?" He gave her a cocky grin.

"Well"—Anne lifted an eyebrow and looked him up and down with languid eyes—"he can sing."

"So can I, darlin'. So can I." With an arm slung around her neck, he steered her out to the Siverado, crooning "Amarillo by Morning" and strumming his imaginary guitar. "Does that turn you on?"

He kept her laughing all the way to the Astrodome. Looking at him now, she wondered how she could have ever been afraid of him. He had brought a whole new dimension, a richness, a delightful abandon to her life that had been missing. Sometimes she wished that this magical interlude could go on and on.

But Vicki was due back any day now. In fact, she was overdue. Knowing that she couldn't trust Spider's phone message to prompt an immediate response from Vicki, she had written a note to her friend, sealed it in a large red envelope, and printed CRITICAL AND CONFIDENTIAL across the front. She had personally delivered it through the mail slot at Vicki's town house several days ago. As soon as Vicki read it, she would call.

In some ways Anne was anxious for Vicki's return; in other ways she dreaded it. Things would change, perhaps irrevocably. She might wish that her carefree time with Spider could stretch into infinity, but her awareness of Preston's threats and crimes never completely abated. Even in the best of times they hovered at the edge of her consciousness, reminding her that she had another life. And responsibilities. She wondered how her gallery was faring. Could Spider ever be a part of that life?

They pulled into the crowded parking area near the Dome, and he stopped the truck.

"Spider?"

"Yes, darlin'?"

"Have you ever considered living someplace else?"

"Besides Houston, you mean?"

She nodded.

He hesitated a moment. "Nah. When I was traded to the Oilers, I was glad to get back home. I imagine I'll hang around here. I'm a Texas boy all the way."

She wanted to ask him how he felt about Virginia, but she didn't. Instead she smiled and said, "Which way to the pigpens?"

"For a city gal, you sure do seem to have a thing for hogs," he teased as he led the way to the livestock exhibit.

The huge Astrohall reeked of cedar fiber and animals, and a cacophony of squawks, grunts, and bleats vied with bellows, snorts, and gobbles.

"All these are part of the junior show," Spider explained as they wandered up and down aisles between pens. He touched his hat and smiled to several people who called out to him. "Kids in 4-H and Future Farmers of America compete for places. Later on in the week, after the judging, the top animals in each class will be auctioned off. The auction is always quite a show."

"Oh, look, there are the pigs," she said, tugging at his arm.

"You don't call them pigs. Those are barrows."

Leaning over a rail, she watched a boy groom the big, snorting animal. "It looks like a pig to me. What's the difference?"

He looked amused. "Well, let's put it this way— these poor fellows can no longer enjoy a sex life. They're destined for bacon and ham and barbecue ribs."

"Spider!" a feminine voice shouted.

They saw a teenaged girl waving from another pen a few yards away. "Hi, Margie," Spider called, steering Anne toward the girl.

He introduced Anne to the pigtailed young lady with a sprinkle of freckles across her nose and said, "Margie had the grand champion barrow last year. Are you going to make it two in a row?"

"I sure hope so," Margie said. "Are you bidding again?"

He grinned. "I thought I might."

To Anne, Margie explained, "Spider bought my barrow last year. It was the highest bid ever made for the class," she added proudly. "Seventy-four thousand dollars."

They chatted a moment longer and walked on, but Anne's brain was still trying to synthesize the information Margie had divulged. "Seventy-four thousand dollars? You paid seventy-four thousand dollars for a neutered pig?"

"I could afford it, and it's good publicity." He shrugged. "Everything over market value is tax-deductible."

"Do I hear another 'and' in there?"

"I'm a sucker for pigtails and freckles."

She narrowed her eyes at him and waited.

"I like ribs."

She raised her eyebrows. "And?"

He shrugged again. "The kid wants to be a veterinarian, and her folks can't afford to send her to college."

"Aha." She grinned. "Spider Webb, you are a teddy bear."

A rush of tender emotion filled her. Her first inclination was to hug him right in the middle of the turkey exhibit. Knowing Spider, he wouldn't have cared, but being the reserved type, she settled for hooking her arm in his and holding on tightly with both hands.

He might be a pawnbroker and live in a converted pizzeria, but she admired Spider more than any man she'd ever known. How many of the men she knew would take time to help an old lady with psychological problems or a young girl who needed a college fund? Oh, they might write a substantial check to charity or attend the high-profile "disease balls" Spider disdained, but how many of them would get personally involved? How many of her friends had been there for her? Not one. It had been Spider, a stranger, who cared enough to help her.

As they strolled through the livestock exhibit, she listened to Spider's running commentary with only part of her attention. With the rest, she wrestled with the question that had plagued her for days: Was she falling in love with Spider, or had she somehow gotten gratitude, excitement, and sexual attraction mixed up with it? As usual, she didn't have an answer.

"Darlin', I get the impression that you're not too excited by the chickens and the steers, and it is pretty ripe in here. Let's go over to the carnival area, and I'll win you a stuffed animal. I think they're more your speed."

"My nose is not that delicate. I grew up with horses, remember? But I would love to have a stuffed animal."

They wandered through the small midway until they found a pitching booth. "Oh, look," she said, pointing to the top row of plush toys. "It's a pig. Isn't he cute?"

"You want one of those?"

She nodded, but after watching several men try their luck with the stacked bottles and walking away empty-handed, she whispered, "Maybe we should forget it. They say these things are rigged."

He patted her hand. "You want a pig, sugar. I'm gonna get you a pig."

It took thirty-seven dollars' worth of balls, but Anne walked away with a fat pink pig under her arm.

They rode the Ferris wheel, ate sausage-on-a-stick and cotton candy, and laughed at the antics of children excited by the festivities. Soon it was time to go inside and see the rodeo, and they followed the flow of the crowd, most of them urban cowboys, through the turnstiles to their places.

Spider kept her close by his side with her arm tucked through his. "I don't want you to get lost in this mob." He grinned down at her. "I think you're as excited about your first rodeo as the kids are."

She laughed. "I am."

Trish and Roscoe were already seated ringside and waved to them as they inched their way to the front row. Lisa and Wally joined them just after the opening ceremony.

"Baby-sitter problems," Lisa explained.

The six of them had a grand time watching the cowboys and cowgirls compete in the various events and cheering for their personal favorites. They groaned with the crowd when a rope missed a steer or when a rider was thrown from a bucking bronco.

Bull riding seemed the most dangerous. Anne thought the few seconds required on a sharp-horned beast's back must feel like forever when the ferocious animal had other ideas. She clutched Spider's arm and hid her face against his shoulder when a mean-looking bull named Thunderbolt wheeled and tried to gore a rider scrambling to get up from the dirt where he'd landed.

He patted her hand. "It's okay, darlin'. The clowns will distract the bull."

Sneaking a peek, she saw that it was true. Two clowns ran out and danced around Thunderbolt, one waving his big red bandanna like a matador's cape, the other pulling the bull's tail. The crowd laughed at the antics of the pair, who diverted the animal's attention from the downed cowboy until he was safely out of the arena.

"Theirs is the most dangerous job," she said as one clown jumped in a blue-and-red barrel milliseconds before a sharp horn would have caught him.

"It can be, but these fellows know what they're doing. I've got a friend who's been a rodeo clown for about ten or twelve years. Would you like to meet him sometime?"

"I'd love to. Has he ever been hurt?"

Spider shrugged. "A couple of times. I'll give him a call next week and—"

He stopped and they looked at one another, both knowing that time was running out. She might not be here next week. By unspoken mutual consent, they changed the direction of their conversation.

Fans in the packed Astrodome were screaming and George Strait had just launched into his second song when Spider's beeper went off.

"Keep my seat warm, sugar, and I'll call to see what Boots wants."

A few minutes later Spider returned with a cardboard tray of beers for the group. As he handed them out, Anne whispered, "Was there an emergency at the shop? Do we need to leave?"

He shook his head. "It'll wait till tomorrow. Let's enjoy the show. Tell me," he said, motioning toward the stage in the arena, "do you really think that guy sings as well as I do?"

Drawing her face into a pose of exaggerated consideration, she cocked her head and studied the beams and glass of the ceiling.

"Well?"

"I'm thinking," she said, "of how I can say this diplomatically."

"Never mind." He laughed and threw his arm around her, drawing her close. "I get the picture."

When George Strait and the Ace in the Hole Band had finished their last encore and left the arena, Wally said, "You guys want to watch some more rodeo, or do you want to go by the Rose and dance for a while?"

Roscoe and Trish wanted to go dancing, and, before Anne could open her mouth to agree, Spider said, "Anne and I are tired. I think we'll call it a night."

"Are you getting old, Spider?" Trish teased. "Or do you two want to be alone?"

He only grinned.

On the way home, he pulled Anne close to him as he drove, tucking her head against his shoulder and setting his chin on the top of her head.

"You seem very quiet," she said. "Are you really tired?"

"No, I just wanted to be with you. Would you rather have gone dancing?"

She gave a contented sigh and settled into the spot where she fit so well. "No."

When he pulled into the strip center and parked in front of the Pawn Parlor's red neon sign, he continued to hold her close to him, making no move to get out of the truck.

"Sugar, I've got something I need to say."

He sounded so serious that Anne's heart lurched and her breath caught. She started to move away so that she could face him, but his arm tightened around her, and his hand pressed her head against his chest and under his cheek. She could feel the thud of his heart, and the dark quiet began to grow ominous.

"I don't know where to start," he said, "except to tell you that I love you."

She gave a little gasp as a mixture of relief and excitement coursed through her. He loved her! "Oh, Spider—"

Laying his fingers on her lips, he said, "Don't say anything, sugar. Let me finish. I know that we haven't known each other very long, but, for me, it's long enough to know that I love you more than anybody or anything in this world. I'm not good at pretty speeches—I wish right now I were—but you've brought sunshine and sweetness into my life, and I don't want to let go of it.

"My bankroll might not measure up to the men's you're used to, but I don't think you'll ever find a man who loves you more than I do. I'd rip out my soul and hand it to you if you wanted it. I know I'd be asking a lot of you to marry someone like me, but if you'd have me, I'd like to make it forever."

"Spider—"

He laid his fingers across her lips again. "Shhh, darlin'. Don't say anything yet. I just want you to think about it. I know you've got a lot on your mind and things are unsettled right now, but I needed to say the words. Remember, whatever happens, I love you with everything that's in me. And as long as I draw a breath, I will cherish you and do everything in my power to keep you safe and happy."

Anne didn't know tears were trickling down her

cheeks until Spider sat her up and brushed them away with his thumbs. "Aw, darlin', don't cry. I didn't mean to upset you."

She sniffed. "You didn't upset me. Spider, you're the dearest, sweetest man in the world. And I lo—"

He silenced her again, but with a brief kiss. Giving her a cocky grin, he said, "I may not be much of a singer, but I'm going to prove to you that nobody can hold a candle to me in a water bed."

"I prefer red satin sheets myself. Vigorous activity in the water bed makes me seasick."

"My bed it is, sugar. I intend to be damned vigorous." He opened the door and dragged her, laughing, from the cab.

"Wait! My pig."

He grabbed the plush pink animal from the seat and stuck it under his arm. In record time, he had the door unlocked and the alarm reset, and to Turk's mellow call of "Step into my parlor, sweet thing," they raced through the shop toward his bedroom.

Spider's hat and jacket landed on the floor. He peeled off Anne's coat and reached for the snaps on her shirt. Laughing, she stilled his hands.

"Why are you in such a hurry, cowboy?"

"I've got a terrible hankerin' for you, ma'am."

"Put your hankerin' on hold for a few minutes, pardner. I'm going to take a shower. I smell like a barnyard."

"You smell like flowers."

He popped three snaps and she wiggled away.

"Spider, I'm going to take a shower." She enunciated each word distinctly.

"Yes, ma'am." He stripped off his shirt and reached for a boot, hopping on one foot as he yanked it off. "I'll take one with you."

Cocking an eyebrow, she smiled. "Why do I get the idea that hygiene is not your primary interest?"

"I can't imagine."

He yanked off his other boot and threw it in a corner by a set of golf clubs. His jeans landed on the organ and his shorts in the lead birdbath.

Magnificently naked, he turned to face her. "Why aren't you undressed, woman?"

Amused, she said, "I was watching the show. Besides, I need help getting my boots off."

"No sooner said than done." He backed her up to the bed and sat her down. Off came the boots. The rest of her clothes followed quickly behind. He grabbed her hand. "To the shower."

She giggled as she trotted along behind him. "Do you always take a shower in your socks?"

"Yeah," he said, not slowing his pace. "Saves on the laundry."

But as soon as the shower was on and the temperature adjusted, he stripped off his socks and tossed them on top of the hamper. Holding open the glass door, he said, "After you, madam."

She stepped inside and picked up the soap. "Uh-uh," he said, taking it from her. "I intend to lather every beautiful inch of your body."

And he did. Some places he lingered longer than others. By the time he was through, her knees felt about as substantial as the soap bubbles. He made a few quick passes over his own body and backed her under the shower head to rinse.

As the warm water sluiced over her shoulders, he bent and took one nipple in his mouth. The sensations of teeth and tongue and lips and water were delightfully erotic. Her back arched and the spray wet her hair and face. His lips drew a trail up to her neck while his hand went lower, to the area he had so painstakingly washed earlier.

While his fingers tested and teased, his tongue led the way as his mouth covered hers in an urgent, aching kiss. Her arms went around him; her fingers slid along his slick, wet body, and she rubbed her breasts against him, savoring the sensation of pelting water, questing tongue, and skin on skin.

She could feel him hot and hard against her stomach, and his hands went to cup her buttocks and lift her to him.

She sucked in a startled breath as she enveloped him. "Oh, Spider."

"Lock your legs around me, sugar," he murmured.

He positioned her so that her back was supported against the tile and the warm spray beat down between them. Thrusting slowly, he brought her to the brink of maddeningly marvelous ecstasy.

"I've never felt anything so wonderful," she murmured. "Oh, Spider, I love you."

"Oh, babe," he groaned and thrust harder, faster.

She cried out as every muscle tensed and sensation shattered her like a million crystal prisms flung into the sun. He, too, cried out and arched. She could feel his love flow into her.

After a few moments, he let her down, tenderly

washed her, and led her from the shower. His eyes, like sparkling blue diamonds, spoke love to her silently as he dried her with a soft towel.

"My hair is wet," she said. "I'll have to dry it."

"Let me." He wrapped her in a bath towel and passed another gently over her head. After he was dry, he draped a towel around his hips, took her into the bedroom, and set her on a stool. He went back for the hair drier and a brush.

With slow, deliberate strokes, he brushed and dried her hair. Eyes closed, she gave over to the rhythmic delight. When the hum of the drier stopped, she opened her eyes. Spider was looking at her with a strange expression that seemed solemn, sad, and loving all at once. She frowned.

"Darlin' "—he took a deep breath—"Vicki called."

Ten

Early the next morning, Spider stood outside of Anne's door and raked his fingers through his hair. He hadn't slept a wink last night after she'd torn a strip off him and flounced out of his room. He felt guilty as hell and sick to his stomach with fear. Maybe, he thought, she'd cooled off some by now. He knocked on the door.

"Anne, are you still mad?"

She flung open the door. "Damned right I'm still mad! I can't believe you didn't tell me right away that Vicki called." She charged down the hall, lugging the eel-skin briefcase with her.

Hot on her heels, he said, "But, darlin', I explained—"

Whirling, she gave him a piercing glare. "I'm tired of your making decisions for me, of your treating me like a fragile flower to be cosseted as if I were a mindless bit of fluff."

"Aw, hell, sugar. I promised I wouldn't do it anymore."

"Yes, but how long will your promise last?" She turned and stalked off.

He grabbed her arm. "Where are you going?"

"To Vicki's, of course."

"I'll go with you."

"You weren't invited. I'm going *alone*."

"At least have some breakfast first."

"Vicki asked me to have breakfast with her." She looked down at his hand encircling her upper arm, then glowered up at him. "If you'll excuse me, I have to call a taxi."

He uttered an abrupt expletive and released her. "At least take the Mercedes. I bought it for you to drive." He held out the keys. "Just be careful."

Hesitating for a moment, she snatched them from his hand. "Thank you. I'm an excellent driver, and I'll take very good care of your car."

"I don't care about the damned car. I care about you. Darlin', please try to understand—"

"We'll discuss this later. Vicki's expecting me."

He let her out the door of the Parlor and stood watching as she drove away. The day he had feared had come. Dread tormented him. Big and ugly and black, it squeezed his heart and ate at his gut. He could feel his life begin to unravel, and there wasn't a damned thing he could do about it.

A tall redhead in a green velour jogging suit opened the door of the town house. She frowned. "Yes?"

Anne looked down at the jeans and sweater she was wearing, patted her blond hair, and grinned. "Don't you recognize me?"

"Anne?"

She laughed. "I'm incognita. My disguise must have worked." Hugging her friend, she said, "Oh, Vicki, I've never been so glad to see anyone in my life. I'm in the world's biggest mess, and I thought you'd never get home."

Vicki pulled her inside. "I'm sorry I wasn't here. One of my most important clients decided to do business while cruising the Caribbean. It played hell with my schedule, but I got a great tan. What's going on with you? Your letter sounded ominous."

While the two curled up on the sofa with coffee, Anne related the events of the past several weeks. When her tale of Preston's duplicity was done, she handed over the briefcase.

Vicki read through the files, then pulled off her reading glasses and tossed them onto the stack of folders on the coffee table. She let out a low whistle. "Heavy stuff. Preston's a real beaut. What do you want to do about it?"

"You're the attorney. I was hoping you would tell me. Obviously, he must be reported to the authorities, but I don't know who to trust. I thought perhaps your father might be able to help."

Vicki unwound her long legs and stood. "Good idea. Pour yourself another cup of coffee and I'll call Dad."

In a few minutes, Vicki was back. She grinned. "I caught him just before he left for a fishing trip. He's going to hop a commuter flight from Dallas and he'll be here in a couple of hours."

"I'm sorry to interrupt his plans."

The redhead laughed. "Are you kidding? Dad's chomping at the bit to get involved. He only retired from his Senate seat because Mom was so ill. He stayed by her side the last few months before she died, but for the past two years, he's been lost without something to do. Oh, he's on the boards of several businesses, but that doesn't fill enough of his time. He misses the activity of Washington. Come on, let's have some breakfast, and you can tell me all about this hunk you're living with."

"How do you know he's a hunk?"

Vicki raised her eyebrow. "Sweetie, every woman in Houston knows who Spider Webb is, and most of them have the hots for him. They watch those crazy commercials of his and lust for his gorgeous body. Lucky girl. I want to hear every delicious detail."

Over breakfast, Anne told her friend about Spider, leaving out most of the delicious details.

Popping a slice of orange into her mouth, Vicki eyed her closely. "You've changed. Not just your appearance—which I like, by the way—but you've got a new spark to your personality. More grit, more life. Is that Spider's doing? Are you in love with him?"

"Sometimes I'm sure I am, and other times I don't know. I've never met anyone quite like him. For all his macho swaggering, he's the most caring person I've ever known. He makes me laugh and he makes me feel sexy. He's generous and fun and stimulating, but he can be the most stubborn, overbearing, infuriating—"

Vicki laughed. "It sounds like love to me. How does he feel?"

Anne sighed. "He says he loves me. He's asked me to marry him."

"And?"

Anne fiddled with her spoon, tracing the design of the silver handle while she examined her feelings. "We come from different worlds. Our backgrounds are just about as far apart as two can be. And we have some problems, primarily over his tendency to be smothering and overprotective. I don't want to turn into the sort of woman my mother was, dependent and little more than an ornament. And I have my gallery in Washington and responsibilities at home to consider."

"Those problems can be worked out if you really love each other."

For the first time, Anne faced her greatest concerns. "I wonder if it is love I feel, a lasting kind of love. Or is it simply an interlude sparked and fed by fear and excitement? And make no mistake, Spider is exciting. One look from him, and I turn into a quivering mass of libido. He rescued me like a dark knight snatching a damsel from the jaws of a dragon. He became my hero. He made me feel things I've never felt before. It's heady, thrilling, deliciously provocative. At the moment. But am I willing to spend the rest of my life living in a pawnshop with a man who only shaves on Saturday? And what about children? What do I want for my children?"

"I think you need some time to decide what's important to you."

Anne met her friend's gaze. "I think you're right."

It was late afternoon when Anne left Vicki and her father. Harmon Chase, a big man with white shaggy eyebrows and a shock of white hair, had arrived on the scene like an avenging angel. The ex-senator, with his sonorous voice and strong sense of justice, was the perfect prototype of the elder statesman.

The three of them had spent hours plotting strategy, and with a few phone calls, Senator Chase had set their plans in motion. A meeting with several high-placed officials was set for the next morning in Washington.

"Now don't you worry about a thing, little lady," the crafty old politician had said as he'd patted her hand. "We'll put that rascal Preston Ames where he belongs and clean up a few other rat's nests while we're at it."

With a suitcase borrowed from Vicki in the seat beside her, Anne headed the Mercedes toward the Pawn Parlor.

"Step into my parlor, sweet thing," Turk's mellow voice invited as she came through the door.

Spider was leaning against the gun case talking to Boots and Molly. Anne managed a bright smile and greeted them. Spider, his face a dark mask, looked down at the suitcase she held, then into her eyes. Only a slight tightening of his jaw betrayed any sign of emotion.

She excused herself and started to her room.

Behind her she heard the heavy stride of boots following her down the hall. She didn't look back.

Laying the suitcase on the water bed, she turned to face Spider. Lounging against the doorjamb, fingers tucked under his armpits, thick brows drawn into a brooding black slash, he waited.

"Going somewhere?"

She sucked in a deep breath and nodded. "To Washington."

"When?"

"Tonight."

"I'm going with you."

"No." Her voice was almost a whisper. "Vicki and her father are going with me."

"You're not going without me."

"Spider, please understand. This is my decision, something I have to do my way."

"When are you coming back?"

She looked away and busied herself opening the suitcase. "I don't know."

He strode toward her and took her in his arms, holding her tightly to him, laying his cheek on top of her head. "Darlin', I don't want you to go. It scares me to think that you might get hurt. If that slimeball gets wind of your whereabouts, he'll try to get to you. Stay here. You'll be safe with me."

She could feel the strong thumping of his heart, and she almost agreed to stay. Almost.

"Spider, I have to go. I'll never really feel safe until Preston is put away. And I can't allow him to continue blackmailing people and abusing my family's estate. He's a menace to others besides me. You know I'm right."

"If you're determined to go, then I'm going, too."

"Don't you ever listen to me? I don't want you to go. I have to do this on my own." She hesitated a moment, then added, "And everything between us has been so crazy and happened so quickly that I think we need some time apart to sort out our feelings."

His arms tightened around her. "I don't need any time. I know how I feel. Annie, I love you. I've never been any more sure of anything in my life. And I'm afraid that if you go without me, you'll forget about me. You'll start mixing with the high-steppers again and never come back."

An ache, deep and smothering, clutched her. The thought that she might never see him again was almost too much to bear. An impulsive, irrational part of her wanted to ask him to forget about the Pawn Parlor and his friends and come with her. They could live in the big house in Virginia, and she had enough money to last for ten lifetimes of extravagance. But would he be happy doing that? She didn't think so. Could she be happy staying here forever? She honestly didn't know.

Pulling back, she looked up into his face. Pain shone from the depths of his crystal-blue eyes. She laid her hand on his cheek. "I could never forget you."

His mouth covered hers in a kiss so fervent that every fiber in her body trembled. As his lips continued to take hers with mounting ferocity, he kicked the door shut, and clothes were shed in desperate urgency. He shoved the suitcase to the floor and laid her on the water bed atop the spread's roses and butterflies.

The aroused tip of her breast shivered, and he took it into his mouth. Fire spread through her as passion flared, burning, blinding.

"You're mine," he said, his voice guttural, husky with emotion. "Mine!"

She answered with a lingering moan, and he captured her in a web of wanting as he touched and laved and kissed her writhing form. His very breath, hot and hard as he groaned her name against desire-stoked skin, set her body blazing until she begged for him.

He plunged into her with a power that launched the bed into great rocking swells. She responded with a demanding rhythm and fierceness that matched his. The roll and pitch of the water bed beneath eager, straining bodies intensified stimulation into an ecstasy of sensation. They rode the great undulating waves as they surged and heaved and broke into a shuddering crest.

When the last shudder was spent, he held her still, murmuring his love for her, dropping tender kisses on her eyes, her nose, her lips. "Come back to me, Annie," he whispered. "Come back to me."

Eleven

The days after her return had been exhausting, physically and emotionally. Anne had told her story countless times and had given depositions until she had become weary of the sound of her own voice. Harmon Chase had been a bulwark of support against the tedium of red tape involved with building a case against Preston. Vicki, too, had been supportive, but the demands of her practice had called her back to Houston the previous week.

Registered under an assumed name and with federal officers guarding her door, Anne sat in the quiet hotel suite gazing out the window at the Washington Monument, its outline hazy through the dismal drizzle, and thinking about Spider. She recalled their last heated lovemaking with bittersweet longing. Three harried weeks had passed, but the memory was still vivid, still evoked a quickening in her body. He'd meant to imprint her with his passion, and he'd succeeded.

Every night she went to her solitary, impersonal hotel bed and ached for his warmth next to her. Yes, he was a magnificent lover, but was sexual compatibility enough for a permanent relationship? No, she reminded herself, it wasn't. She remembered that Betsy Carmichael had come home after the flame had burned out with her Oregon dream man. They were simply too different. It had bothered him that Betsy had piles of money, and she hadn't been willing to give it up. In the end, he'd started drinking and their romance had ended.

Would Spider be any different? Was what they had something more stable? Or had it been a temporary fling born of her desperation and fear? She didn't know. But what she did know was that she needed time, and she needed to learn to be independent.

Yet when the lock rattled, for one illogical minute she hoped it was Spider coming to throw her over his shoulder and take her back to Houston with him. Her face fell as a smiling Harmon Chase strode into the room.

"It's official. Preston's been indicted, and he's locked up tighter than Dick's hatband. No bond. The list of charges against him is longer than my arm—everything from attempted murder to a wad of federal offenses that would choke a horse. We can dismiss that pair of government gumshoes outside, and you can go home."

Anne gave a sigh of relief and smiled. "It's over."

"Everything but the formality of the trial." He slapped his hands together. "Damnation, it feels good to be useful again! I'm going to go call Vicki. She's going to be sorry she went home last week and missed the big moment."

He strode to his bedroom and closed the door. Her first impulse was to call Spider. She stilled her hand before it could pick up the receiver. Time. She needed time.

While Harmon and a team of auditors started through Preston's papers trying to get things straightened out, Anne rattled around in her big house on the hill. Her footsteps echoed down empty hallways, and there was no one to talk to except servants, who were busy with their work and at a loss as to what to say to their employer. She wandered from one room to the next, picking up an item here and there and replacing it in its precise spot. The rooms where she'd spent her entire life seemed cold and too well ordered. They had no personality.

Walking over the grounds where she'd played as a child, she discovered that the familiar was suddenly alien and lonely. She sat on the stone bench and stared at the rosebushes, freshly pruned and mulched. The first signs of spring growth colored the thorny canes, and, before long, fragrant blossoms would appear. But there was no one to enjoy them except the gardener and her.

She missed Spider and her new friends and the excitement she'd found in Houston. Dear Lord, she was bored, and she'd only been home for an afternoon.

In her pristine bedroom, she dressed in an Ungaro gown and went to the club for dinner. Most of the people there hadn't even realized she'd been away, but several women complimented her dress. She knew that everyone in the room was dying to know the juicy details of Preston's perfidy but were too polite to inquire directly.

A few supposed friends of long standing, whose help she had solicited the night she'd escaped from Preston, made sheepish comments about being shocked at the news of his duplicity. She tried to smile and say the right things. Those she spoke with seemed strangely superficial and synthetic, the type who gussied up and went to disease balls. Oddly, she'd never noticed before. They were bland when compared to Spider.

Even the food, expertly prepared by a French chef, was tasteless. She suddenly craved barbecued ribs and beer. And a man who wore a gold-filled spider in his ear. Excusing herself from the acquaintances she'd joined for dinner, she went home. She doubted if they'd miss her.

After a restless night, she drove to her gallery in Washington.

Walking into the chic establishment off Dupont Circle, she spied Meg, the woman she'd called a friend, showing a Victorian watercolor to a blue-haired matron with a Pekingese under her arm. The woman and her beribboned dog looked remarkably similar—haughty and pampered with a pug nose and a serious underbite.

Meg, who managed the gallery for Anne, was dressed in a black Adolfo with a triple strand of pearls and her dark hair tied back with a big velvet bow. When she spotted Anne, dressed in jeans, a casual blue sweater, and Reeboks, Meg looked her up and down, then dismissed her as she turned back to the matron with a fawning smile.

Anger boiled up inside her. Her fingers itched to yank that big black bow from Meg's perfectly coiffed hair and stomp on it. She had the greatest urge to march over to her fair-weather friend and slap her silly.

Instead, she balled her fingers into fists and said sharply, "Meg, I need to speak with you. Now."

Meg wheeled around, her eyes wide. "Anne?"

"Yes."

Meg turned the customer over to her assistant, Jacob, and hurried over. "Oh, Anne, thank Heaven you're here. Reporters have been calling all morning. What have you done to yourself? I didn't recognize you. Are you all right? Howard and I were stunned when we read the Post this morning. It's unbelievable." Only a slight tremor at the upper corner of her red lips betrayed any emotion. "I hope you're not upset with Howard and me. That night you came to the house, we didn't know what to do, and, after all, Preston was Howard's employer. I'm sure you can understand his awkward position."

As Meg chattered on, Anne looked at her with new eyes. This shallow woman had never been her friend. Even now her only concern was a selfish one.

"Royal Fox was Howard's employer, Meg. The operative word is *was*. And *I* own Royal Fox Hotels, not Preston."

Meg went pale. "Why, Anne dear, what do you mean?"

"I mean that your husband is, to quote a dear friend of mine, a slimeball, and I'm kicking him out."

Blood-red lips parted in a feral snarl. "Why, you little twit! I wish Preston *had* found you."

Anne raised an eyebrow. "You're fired, too, Meg. I've overpaid you too long. Get your things and get out. Now."

As Meg flounced away in a huff, Anne heard a snort from behind her. Turning, she saw Jacob trying to wipe the smile from his face. The lady with the Pekingese was gone, and obviously Jacob had heard most of their conversation.

"How do you feel about my firing Meg, Jacob?"

A tiny smile crept back. "It couldn't have happened to a more deserving person."

"It occurs to me that you probably do most of the real work around here. Do you think you can manage the gallery?"

The smile spread to a grin. "Hell, yes—I mean— certainly, Miss Jennings."

She returned his grin. " 'Hell, yes' will do nicely. In fact, I don't have any use for it where I'm going. I think I'm going to give it to you."

His eyes grew big as silver dollars. "*Give* it to me?"

"'Yep. The gallery is yours."

As she turned and strode to the door, he called after her, "Miss Jennings, where are you going?"

She laughed. "Why, sugar, I'm going to Texas."

It was almost nine o'clock when she drove into the strip center and parked in front of the red neon sign. She left her bags in the car she'd rented at the airport and walked to the door. Her finger trembled as she pushed the button.

When she heard the click of the lock, she went in. She was nervous. Very nervous. What if Spider had changed his mind? She should have called.

"Step into my parlor, sweet thing. Let ol' Spider help you out."

Anne smiled at the myna's greeting, then started picking her way around the merchandise. Very little had changed. Even the smells were the same as she'd remembered.

"Hot damn!" a deep voice shouted over the crowd roaring on TV.

"Hot damn," Turk agreed.

She chuckled as she circled the wooden Indian and the drum set, heading for the back of the shop. She froze in her tracks when she saw him.

He was leaning against one of the glass cases. Arms crossed and fingers tucked under his armpits, his face was shadowed with several days' growth of black beard. He wore black boots, black jeans, a black T-shirt, and a little gold spider in his left ear.

His eyes were narrowed under the thick slash of black eyebrows and his sensuously curving mouth was solemn, but she could feel those blue eyes slither over her. She could feel the desire emanating from them low within her. It stole her breath and hardened her nipples. It made her legs go weak and her heart pound.

She licked her lips. He licked his.

"Spider . . ." Her voice was barely a whisper.

One corner of his mouth slowly lifted into a sensual smile. "You need a little cash tonight, sugar?"

He walked toward her, and the scent of him filled her nostrils. Citrus and sandalwood and virile male. They stood inches apart, not touching but searching one another's eyes.

"How much will you give me for my watch?"

He smiled and lifted one finger to rub along the curve of her cheek. "Everything I've got, darlin'. Everything I've got."

"A funny thing happened to me while I was away. I discovered that my old life was very boring. And very lonely."

"I know the feeling, sugar." His finger trailed along the edge of her jaw to her chin.

"Preston is in jail."

"I read about it."

"Oh, Spider, I love you. Do you still want—"

His arms went around her and his mouth covered hers with a heart-stopping kiss. The ferocity of his lips and tongue and the snarl reverberating deep in his throat told her everything she wanted to know. Knees weak, she clung to him as he kissed her, as he nipped and nuzzled her neck.

"Oh, darlin', I was scared to death you weren't coming back. I love you. And I've missed you so much," he murmured as he continued to hold her close to him.

"Spider, I don't want my money to come between us. I'll give it all to charity if it bothers you."

He pulled back and looked at her as if she'd lost her mind. "That's the craziest damned thing I've ever heard. Darlin', I've told you a dozen times, I don't give a hoot if you have more money than Donald Trump. If it doesn't bother you, it doesn't bother me."

"Are you sure? I've got a hell of a bundle."

He threw back his head and laughed. "I love you, sugar. Money, warts, and all."

She pursed her lips. "I don't have any warts."

He laughed and kissed her again. "I've got a couple. Are you willing to marry me?"

"On one condition. Will you please back off a little and stop being so overprotective? Will you ask me before you charge in and make my decisions for me?"

"I promise I'll do my very best. And if I forget, you have my permission to remind me with a baseball bat."

She smiled. "Then, yes, I'll marry you."

"Hot damn!" He picked her up and strode down the hall toward his bedroom.

"What are you doing?" she squealed as he dragged her sweater over her head.

He unzipped her jeans. "I'm about to make love to you all night and into next week."

Her eyes narrowed and her fists went to her hips.

His hands stilled and he cleared his throat. "If that's okay with you, sugar."

She studied the ceiling a moment, then grinned. "It is. I've been dreaming about red satin sheets."

Epilogue

As Spider drove the Silverado home, Anne sat snuggled next to him. "I think the rodeo this year was even better than last year's," she said, stifling a yawn. "Don't you?"

"Ummm," he replied. "Are you sure you didn't get too tired?"

"Positive. Don't fuss so." She patted his thigh. "And this year *I* bought the championship barrow. They said it was the highest price ever paid."

He laughed. "Sugar, for the last five raises, nobody was bidding against you but me."

"Why did you do that?"

"I thought you were getting a kick out of it. Besides, you need the tax deduction."

After he'd wheeled the black pickup into the driveway of the suburban house, Anne poked the button of a remote-control unit and the double doors of the garage went up. He pulled in beside a blue Mercedes and helped her out of the cab. Arm in arm, they walked through the house, a sprawling ranch style with a swimming pool, and into the den. The LeRoy Neiman football painting hung on one wall and the wooden Indian stood by the fireplace.

"You know," she said, looking around the comfortably furnished room, with its high-beamed ceiling and oversize furniture, "sometimes I miss living at the Pawn Parlor."

Spider laughed and rubbed her big tummy. "We couldn't bring up Scooter here in a pawnshop."

She laid her hand over his. "I feel like such a blimp. How can you still love me when I'm so fat?"

He kissed her nose. "Darlin', I'd love you if you weighed six hundred pounds and had green hair."

"My money really hasn't been a problem, has it?"

"Nah," he said. "I told you it wouldn't bother me. How many husbands have a wife who'd give them a football team for Christmas?"

She laughed. "Harmon nearly croaked. He's taking his job of managing my affairs very seriously. And he loves living near Washington again. Vicki says he seems ten years younger."

They walked to the large master bedroom, which sported high ceilings and another fireplace. Amid the tastefully appointed furnishings sat a king-size brass bed with red satin sheets and a fake-fur spread. He sat on the side of it and drew her into his lap, holding her close and rubbing her belly.

"I'll be glad when Junior has his birthday. I've got a terrible hankering for his mama."

She pressed his head against her breast, ran her fingers through his thick hair, and caressed his cheek. She touched the familiar spider earring, an eighteen-karat gold one, and kissed his forehead. "I've got a terrible hankering for his papa, too. Does it bother you very much?"

"Nah, I'll live. You want a glass of milk or something, sugar?"

She shook her head, then stiffened in his arms.

"What's the matter, darlin'?"

"I'm not sure, but I think I just had a labor pain."

"Omigod!" Spider sprang to his feet with Anne in his arms and started running through the house.

"Spider Webb! What are you *doing*?"

"I'm taking you to the hospital."

She laughed. "Put me down, you idiot. I'm not even sure it was a labor pain. And if it was, it will be hours yet. I have to pack my bag and call the doctor."

He ran back into their bedroom and laid her down on the fur spread. "Don't move. I'll pack your bag. Where is it?"

"In my closet. I'll get it."

His wild blue eyes narrowed to thin slits beneath his black slashing brows, and he held up his hand in a signal to stop. "Don't you move a foot off that bed. I'll handle this."

She smiled as he strode around the room, dragging things out of drawers and cramming them into her suitcase. He was still overprotective—he would probably always be—but her heart was filled almost to bursting with love for him.

With his father assisting and muttering obscenities at the doctor every time his mother had a labor pain, William Andrew Webb, Jr. was born in Cypress Creek Hospital at 6:43 A.M. Twenty-two and a half inches long, he weighed eight pounds and four ounces, had blue eyes, a full head of black hair, and a wicked smile that the doctor declared was only a gas bubble. The nurses said he had the strongest lungs and the biggest hands and feet of any baby in the nursery.

THE EDITOR'S CORNER

Those sultry June breezes will soon start to whisper through the trees, bringing with them the wonderful scents of summer. Imagine the unmistakable aroma of fresh-cut grass and the feeling of walking barefoot across a lush green lawn. Then look on your bookstore shelves for our striking jade-green LOVESWEPTs! The beautiful covers next month will put you right in the mood to welcome the summer season—and our authors will put you in the mood for romance.

Peggy Webb weaves her sensual magic once more in **UNTIL MORNING COMES,** LOVESWEPT #402. In this emotional story, Peggy captures the stark beauty of the Arizona desert and the fragile beauty of the love two very different people find together. In San Francisco he's known as Dr. Colter Gray, but in the land of his Apache ancestors, he's Gray Wolf. Reconciling the two aspects of his identity becomes a torment to Colter, but when he meets Jo Beth McGill, his life heads in a new direction. Jo Beth has brought her elderly parents along on her assignment to photograph the desert cacti. Concerned about her father's increasing senility, Jo Beth has vowed never to abandon her parents to the perils of old age. But when she meets Colter, she worries that she'll have to choose between them. When Colter appears on his stallion in the moonlight, ready to woo her with ancient Apache love rituals, Jo Beth trembles with excitement and gives herself up to the mysterious man in whose arms she finds her own security. This tender story deals with love on many levels and will leave you with a warm feeling in your heart.

In LOVESWEPT #403 by Linda Cajio, all it takes is **JUST ONE LOOK** for Remy St. Jacques to fall for the beguiling seductress Susan Kitteridge. Ordered to shadow the woman he believes to be a traitor, Remy comes to realize the lady who drives him to sweet obsession could not be what she seemed. Afraid of exposing those she loves to danger, Susan is caught up in the life of lies she'd live for so long. But she yearns to confess all to Remy the moment the bayou outlaw captures her lips with his. In her smooth, sophisticated style, Linda creates a winning love story you won't be able to put down. As an added treat, Linda brings back the lovable character of Lettice as her third and last granddaughter finds true happiness and love. Hint! Hint! This won't be the last you'll hear of Lettice, though. Stay tuned!

(continued)

With her debut book, **PERFECT MORNING**, published in April 1989, Marcia Evanick made quite a splash in the romance world. Next month Marcia returns to the LOVESWEPT lineup with **INDESCRIBABLY DELICIOUS**, LOVESWEPT #404. Marcia has a unique talent for blending the sensuality of a love story with the humorous trials and tribulations of single parenthood. When Dillon McKenzie follows a tantalizing scent to his neighbor's kitchen, he finds delicious temptation living next door! Elizabeth Lancaster is delighted that Dillon and his two sons have moved in; now her boy Aaron will have playmates. What she doesn't count on is becoming Dillon's playmate! He brings out all her hidden desires and makes her see there's so much more to life than just her son and the business she's built creating scrumptious cakes and candies. You'll be enthralled by these two genuine characters who must find a way to join their families as well as their dreams.

As promised, Tami Hoag returns with her second pot of pure gold in *The Rainbow Chasers* series, **KEEPING COMPANY**, LOVESWEPT #405. Alaina Montgomery just knew something would go wrong on her way to her friend Jayne's costume party dressed as a sexy comic-book princess. When her car konks out on a deserted stretch of road, she's more embarrassed by her costume than frightened of danger—until Dylan Harrison stops to help her. At first she believes he's an escaped lunatic, then he captivates her with his charm and incredible sex appeal—and Alaina actually learns to like him—even after he gets them arrested. A cool-headed realist, Alaina is unaccustomed to Dylan's care-free attitude toward life. So she surprises even herself when she accepts his silly proposal to "keep company" to curtail their matchmaking friends from interfering in their lives. Even more surprising is the way Dylan makes her feel, as if her mouth were made for long, slow kisses. Tami's flare for humor shines in this story of a reckless dreamer who teaches a lady lawyer to believe in magic.

In Judy Gill's **DESPERADO**, LOVESWEPT #406, hero Bruce Hagendorn carries the well-earned nickname of Stud. But there's much more to the former hockey star than his name implies—and he intends to convince his lovely neighbor, Mary Delaney, of that fact. After Mary saves him from a severe allergy attack that she had unintentionally caused, Bruce vows to coax his personal Florence Nightingale out to play. An intensely driven woman, Mary has set certain goals

(continued)

for herself that she's focused all her attention on attaining—doing so allows her to shut out the hurts from her past. But Bruce/Stud won't take no for an answer, and Mary finds herself caught under the spell of the most virile man she's ever met. She can't help wishing, though, that he'd tell her where he goes at night, what kind of business it is that he's so dedicated to. But Bruce knows once he tells Mary, he could lose her forever. This powerful story is sure to have an impact on the lives of many readers, as Judy deals with the ecstasy and the heartache true love can bring.

We're delighted as always to bring you another memorable romance from one of the ladies who's helped make LOVESWEPT so successful. Fayrene Preston's *SwanSea Place:* **DECEIT**, LOVESWEPT #407, is the *pièce de résistance* to a fabulous month of romantic reading awaiting you. Once again Fayrene transports you to Maine and the great estate of SwanSea Place, where Richard Zagen has come in search of Liana Marchall, the only woman he's ever loved. Richard has been haunted, tormented by memories of the legendary model he knows better as the heartless siren who'd left him to build her career in the arms of another. Liana knows only too well the desperate desire Richard is capable of making her feel. She's run once from the man who could give her astonishing pleasure and inflict shattering pain, but time has only deepened her hunger for him. Fayrene's characters create more elemental force than the waves crashing against the rocky coast. Let them sweep you up in their inferno of passion!

As always we invite you to write to us with your thoughts and comments. We hope your summer is off to a fabulous start!
Sincerely,

Susann Brailey

Susann Brailey
Editor
LOVESWEPT
Bantam Books
666 Fifth Avenue
New York, NY 10103

FAN OF THE MONTH

Ricki L. Ebbs

I guess I started reading the LOVESWEPT series as soon as it hit the market. I had been looking for a different kind of romance novel, one that had humor, adventure, a little danger, some offbeat characters, and, of course, true love and a happy ending. When I read my first LOVESWEPT, I stopped looking.

Fayrene Preston, Kay Hooper, Iris Johansen, Joan Elliott Pickart, Sandra Brown, and Deborah Smith are some of my favorite authors. I love Kay Hooper's wonderful sense of humor. For pure sensuality, Sandra Brown's books are unsurpassed. Though their writing styles are different, Iris Johansen, Joan Elliott Pickart, and Fayrene Preston write humorous, touching, and wonderfully sentimental stories. Deborah Smith's books have a unique blend of adventure and romance, and she keeps bringing back those characters I always wonder about at the end of the story. (I'm nosy about my friends' lives too.)

I'm single, with a terrific but demanding job as an administrative assistant. When I get the chance, I always pick up a mystery or romance novel. I have taken some kidding from my family and friends for my favorite reading. My brother says I should have been Sherlock Holmes or Scarlett O'Hara. I don't care what they say. I may be one of the last romantics, but I think the world looks a little better with a slightly romantic tint, and LOVESWEPTs certainly help to keep it rosy.

THE DELANEY DYNASTY

THE SHAMROCK TRINITY

- ☐ 21975 RAFE, THE MAVERICK
  by Kay Hooper $2.95
- ☐ 21976 YORK, THE RENEGADE
  by Iris Johansen $2.95
- ☐ 21977 BURKE, THE KINGPIN
  by Fayrene Preston $2.95

THE DELANEYS OF KILLAROO

- ☐ 21872 ADELAIDE, THE ENCHANTRESS
  by Kay Hooper $2.75
- ☐ 21873 MATILDA, THE ADVENTURESS
  by Iris Johansen $2.75
- ☐ 21874 SYDNEY, THE TEMPTRESS
  by Fayrene Preston $2.75

THE DELANEYS: *The Untamed Years*

- ☐ 21899 GOLDEN FLAMES *by Kay Hooper* $3.50
- ☐ 21898 WILD SILVER *by Iris Johansen* $3.50
- ☐ 21897 COPPER FIRE *by Fayrene Preston* $3.50

THE DELANEYS II

- ☐ 21978 SATIN ICE *by Iris Johansen* $3.50
- ☐ 21979 SILKEN THUNDER *by Fayrene Preston* $3.50
- ☐ 21980 VELVET LIGHTNING *by Kay Hooper* $3.50
